The Other Side of Me

Also by K. A. Last

Fiction
Sacrifice – A Fall For Me Prequel
(The Tate Chronicles, #0.5)
Bound (The Tate Chronicles, #0.6)
Fall For Me (The Tate Chronicles, #1)
Fight For Me (The Tate Chronicles, #2)
Die For Me (The Tate Chronicles, #3)
The Tate Chronicles Omnibus
Immagica
The Lovely Dark
Something (All the Things: part one)
Nothing (All the Things: part two)
Everything (All the Things: part three)
All the Things (Something, Nothing, Everything)

Non-fiction
The Tate Chronicles Notebook
Immagica Notebook
A Novel Idea! Colouring Journal for Writers

K. A. LAST

www.kalastbooks.com.au

K. A. Last
kalast@kalastbooks.com.au
www.kalastbooks.com.au

ISBN: 978-0-6480257-8-8

Formatting and cover design by KILA Designs
www.kiladesigns.com.au
Cover images: ©bigstockphoto.com

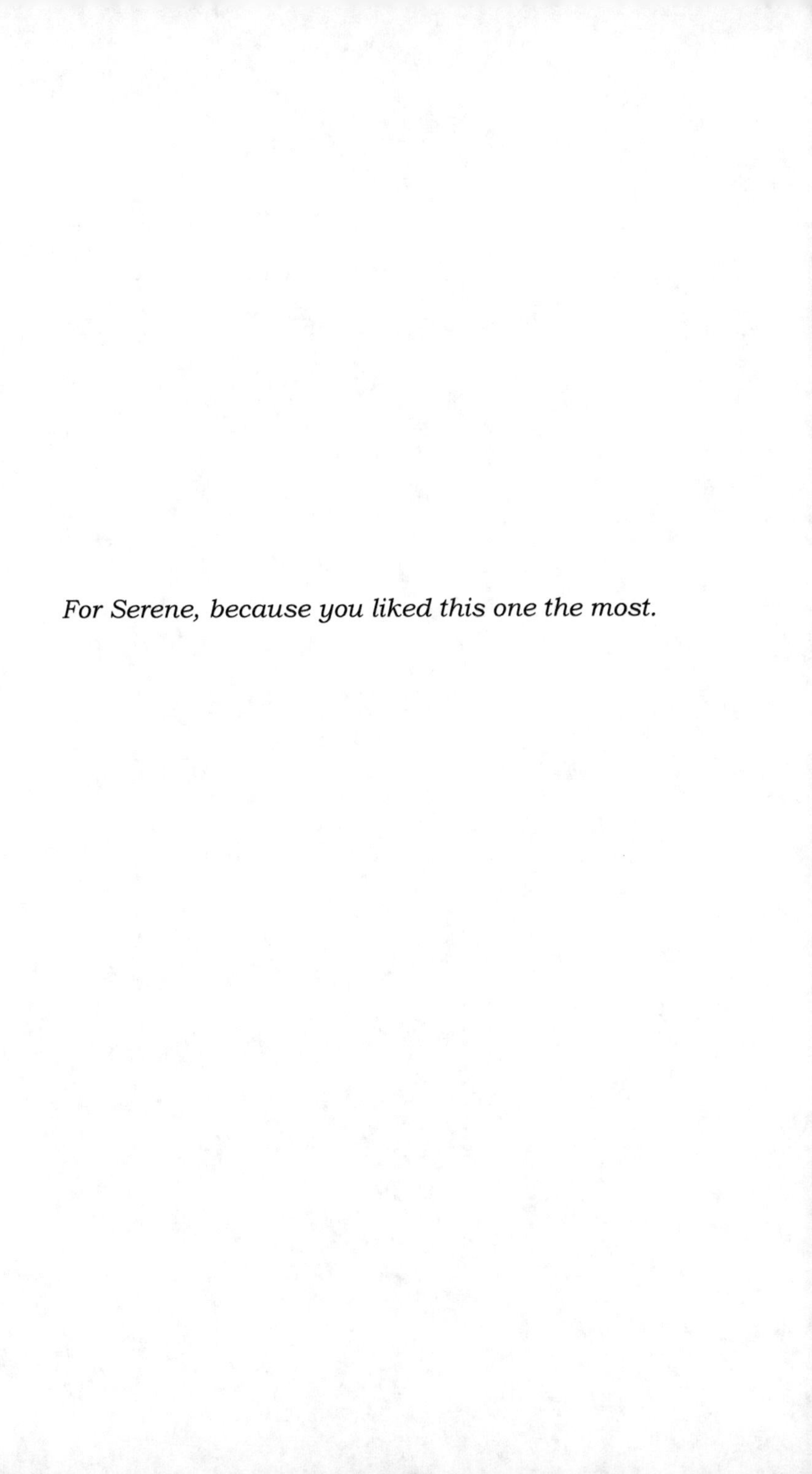

For Serene, because you liked this one the most.

Contents

This One?

The sliding doors open, and the noise of the airport hits me as Stacey and I step through. It's been a long and eventful week in Surfers Paradise, and I'm glad to finally be going home.

I spot my sister, Josephine, and her friends sitting off to the side of the terminal, a pile of bags and backpacks at their feet. Levi glances up and smiles, then nudges Josephine who waves us over.

"I hope Katie and Levi sort everything out," I say to Stacey.

She looks at the group of kids who aren't really our friends, but who tolerate us because Josephine is my twin sister, and Levi is Katie's boyfriend. I think.

"I'm sure they will," Stacey replies. "Everything will be perfect when we get home. You'll see."

Josephine waves at us again, and I grip the handle of my suitcase, moving towards her.

"We don't have to go sit with them." Stacey touches my arm. "You are allowed to be separated from Josie for more than five minutes."

"I know. But what else do we have to do?" I shrug. "Our flight is after theirs. We may as well go talk to them."

Despite the fact my sister can be a bitch, and her friends are the popular snobby rich kids, I still love her. She's my best friend.

"We have to check our bags first," Stacey says.

I wave at Josephine then point to the check-in counters. She gives me a thumbs-up as Stacey grabs my arm and pulls me in the opposite direction. The line moves quickly, and five minutes later we're two suitcases lighter.

I head towards my sister and her friends, and Stacey follows me to where Josephine sits beside Levi. The rest of the gang are here, too. Veronica, Rachel, Jarred, and Geoff. We've all been through a lot this year, and I hope everyone has been able to get some perspective after finally finishing high school, and being away from our parents for a week.

Levi perches on the edge of his seat, staring at me.

"Katie is fine." I drop my backpack at my feet, knowing he wants to ask me about her.

Veronica smacks Levi on the arm. "Didn't you see her this morning?"

"Dude, you're whipped." Jarred grins.

Josephine throws him a dirty look, and he laughs.

Levi shrugs. "I want to make sure she's okay after last night."

"She's just as okay as she was when you said goodbye to her." Stacey drops into the seat on the end of the row. "We need a group photo. Geoff, you can take it. Come on girls, gather round."

Rachel scrunches her nose up. Veronica goes and sits beside Stacey. The rest of us girls form a group, and Rachel reluctantly follows.

"If the wind changes, your face will stay like that," Karen says to Rachel.

"Smile, girls." Geoff holds his phone up. "Done. At ease, Rach."

Josephine jumps up from her chair. "I need to pee."

"Charming," Rachel snorts, popping her gum.

I raise my eyebrows and she smirks.

Would our flight hurry up already?

"Come with me." Josephine grabs her bag then tugs my hand.

She nods at me eagerly, so I snare the strap of my backpack as she pulls me away, slinging it over my shoulder.

"Why do girls always have to pee together?" Geoff calls, and my cheeks heat.

Safety in numbers. Memories from the week flood my mind. Katie being assaulted by that guy, Scott. Geoff of all people helping her.

I shake it off and follow my sister into the ladies toilets. Josephine checks under all the stall doors.

"Good, no one's here." She straightens. "Let's swap."

"Huh?" I stare at her. "You said you needed to pee."

"Come on, Jess." She stands with her hands on her hips. "Let's twin swap."

I continue to stare, opening my mouth to say something, then closing it.

"Have you forgotten how to talk?" Josephine asks.

I open my mouth again, and a puff of air comes out. "Josie, twin swapping is never a good idea. We know from experience."

Josephine twirls a lock of her blonde hair around her finger. "You are so boring."

"And you're insane."

"Come on, Jess. It'll be fun to try to trick our friends."

"They'll know," I say. "Stacey will pick you a mile away."

"I bet she won't. I'm a very good actress." Josephine puts her hand in the air and twirls. She's wearing Converse sneakers and denim shorts, and the sight makes me laugh. She's the furthest thing from a ballerina. "Come on, I dare you."

"Oh no. No way. I've learnt my lesson with that stupid game," I say. "After everything that's happened with Katie, truth or dare should be outlawed."

"I've never known you to back down from a dare." Josephine wiggles her eyebrows.

"What if I said I don't want to?" I ask, leaning against the sink. "We've had enough drama with Katie and Veronica over the past few months. Why add fuel to the fire?"

"Why not?" Josephine shrugs, then gives me this look she has given me ever since we were little. The look that says, *I'm your sister and you should do this because I asked you to and you love me.*

We stare at each other. Josephine with her head cocked to the side and her eyes pleading. Me with my arms folded over my chest.

"You try being around my friends all the time," she says, breaking the silence. "I need some space."

"You love your friends." I frown.

"Yeah, but they're exhausting, and Jarred ..." She glances at her feet.

"What did he do? Did he hurt you?"

"No, of course not." Josephine looks at me again. "I just ... Come on, Jess."

"As long as you tell me what's wrong when we get home. Because I know you, and something is bothering you."

"I promise." Josephine reaches out and squeezes my hand. "We can make popcorn, and stay up all night talking if you like."

"Fine," I say.

"You're the best." My sister grins and hugs me.

I hug her back. "But let it go on the record I think this is a bad idea."

There must be something going on between Josephine and Jarred if she wants to swap with me. Or there's another reason besides wanting space from her friends. But I don't ask her any more questions. I figure she'll tell me what's wrong when she's ready. That's the way we've always been. If I push her too hard for answers to anything, she shuts down. Especially when something is bugging her. It's better to let her tell me in her own time.

We go into the disabled stall and switch clothes and shoes, before transferring all our stuff and swapping bags. Josephine pulls my hair out of its ponytail and ties hers back with the elastic. She grabs some toilet paper and wets it with water from the little sink on the wall, using it to wipe most of the makeup from her face. Then

she pulls out her cosmetic purse and quickly applies some foundation, eyeshadow, and mascara to my face and eyes.

"Gloss." She hands me her favourite pink tube.

I dab it on my lips and smack them together. "This stuff is gross. It makes my lips sticky."

Josephine takes the gloss and puts it back in her makeup bag. She hands it to me. "Take this. I don't need it being you." She grins. "And you should wear more makeup."

"You should wear less." I take the small cosmetic purse and tuck it into my bag, licking my lips. They taste like strawberry. "You're beautiful without it."

"Stand up straight," Josephine says, ignoring my compliment. "I don't slouch."

"I know how to be you."

"Let's go then."

"Hang on." I touch her arm. "What about … Jarred?"

"What about him?" Josephine shrugs again.

"What if … you know? He tries to kiss me or something?"

"Just push him away. I do it all the time."

I frown. "Is everything okay with you?" *Because I don't think it is.*

"We're fine." Josephine twists her ponytail around her finger.

"Stop doing that. Twisting your hair. It's a Josie thing, not a Jess thing."

Josephine rolls her eyes. "I know how to be you, Jess."

"This is a bad idea."

"Just … go with it and have fun."

Josephine opens the stall door and we step out into

the main part of the public toilets. Two girls stand at the basins, but thankfully we don't know them. It's on the tip of my tongue to ask Josephine again why she wants to do this, but I don't. I guess it could be fun to see if we can pull it off, since we haven't tried something like this on our friends in a long time.

Go with it. Have fun.

We wash our hands, then I take a deep breath and follow my sister out to where the others are seated. I almost go and sit with Stacey, but remember just in time that I'm supposed to be Josephine, so I dump my bag and sit on Jarred's lap.

"How much longer until our flight?" I whine in my best Josephine voice.

Jarred wraps his arms around my middle and nuzzles into my neck. "Not long."

His embrace feels better than I expected. If Josephine wants to play this game, I may as well enjoy the good parts.

"Get a room you two," Veronica says.

"Yeah, Josie," Josephine says.

I look over at my sister, the real Josephine, and she's scowling. I raise my eyebrows and twirl a lock of hair around my finger. I can't tell if she's pissed off because I'm sitting on Jarred's lap, or because I do her better than she does herself.

Maybe I should ease up a little. I use getting a bottle of water from my bag as a reason to stand. Then I sit back beside Jarred instead of on top of him.

I watch Josephine from the corner of my eye while I listen to Veronica and Rachel chat about the past week. Jarred rubs circles on my leg, and I hate how good it

makes me feel, because it shouldn't make me feel anything. I'm not his girlfriend, but he thinks I am.

I've never had a real boyfriend. When Josephine started going out with Jarred, I was jealous. I've had a crush on him for years, but I've never told anyone. Quiet little Jessica doesn't spill secrets like that.

Guilt washes through me because I'm enjoying Jarred's touch, and I want to jump up and tell everyone we've tricked them. Tell Josephine we've gone far enough. But when I make eye contact with her she smiles, and I see myself in her as if I'm looking into a mirror.

If she wanted to end this now, she would. Nothing ever stops Josephine from saying exactly what she wants to. Mostly Veronica's influence, I think.

We all sit and wait. Half an hour feels like eternity, and when a voice comes over the PA system announcing that Josephine's flight is boarding, I sit up straighter in my seat, eager to get this over with.

My gaze connects with my sister's, and she smiles at me in a way that is identical to how I've smiled at myself in the mirror so many times. There's a sad edge to it, and I briefly wonder if I look that sad all the time.

"Get up, bitches," Veronica says, standing. "I've had enough of Queensland." She shoulders her bag and digs out her boarding pass.

I do the same, only the pass I'm holding is for my original flight, not Josephine's.

Crap.

The group walk towards the gate. I give Josephine a hug.

"What's up with you two freaks?" Stacey asks. "You'll

see each other in a few hours."

I pat Josephine on the back and give her a squeeze. "Boarding passes," I whisper in her ear.

When I pull away, Josephine's eyes are wider than usual, but she keeps herself in check.

"Josie," Veronica calls. "Hurry up."

My sister and I both look at her standing in the middle of the concourse.

"Can you give me that book?" Josephine asks, turning back to me and raising her eyebrows. "The one I lent you?"

Josephine knows I always have a book in my bag, so I dig around in the bag I'm holding—her bag, which now has my stuff in it—and slip my boarding pass inside the cover before pulling it out. She lifts her hand to take it, and a piece of paper flutters to the ground.

Josephine bends to pick it up with her free hand. "You might need this to get on the plane."

"You think?" I say, emulating Josephine's tone.

I roll my eyes like she does so often, and take the boarding pass from her, glancing at the flight number. It's her flight. The one I'm supposed to be getting on right now with her boyfriend and friends.

What are we doing?

"I'll see you at home." I take off towards Veronica and the others.

"Stay safe," Josephine calls in her best Jessica voice.

She sounds so much like me it's scary. I wave at her over my shoulder, but don't look back, jogging to Veronica's side. She glances at me as we walk fast to catch up to the rest of the group already waiting to board the plane.

"Everything okay with you?" Veronica asks.

"Yeah, all good." I flick my hair over my shoulder like Josephine does, and don't say anything else. I figure if I don't talk too much I'll have a better chance of not being found out.

We fall into line with the others, and Jarred puts an arm around my shoulders. I smile up at him, then check my expression and change it to what I hope is more of a sexy stare.

Being my sister is exhausting.

He kisses my forehead and we shuffle along the line, get our boarding passes scanned, then follow the ramp onto the plane.

Jarred gives me the window seat, so I buckle myself in, put my bag under the seat in front of me, and settle in for the short flight back to Sydney. Geoff and Levi are behind us, and Veronica and Rachel are in the two seats in front.

Veronica kneels in her seat and looks over the back of it at me. "Great week, huh?"

"Sure." I smile up at her, hoping she's not going to reminisce over anything I wasn't there for.

"Especially Wednesday night."

From the corner of my eye I catch Jarred looking at me. His stare makes my cheeks heat. The burning creeps down my neck.

I hold Veronica's gaze, and a moment passes between us. "It was the best."

I have no idea what they, or Josephine, did on Wednesday night, but it's obvious Veronica has caught me out. I wait for her to call me on it, but she doesn't.

"Are you sure you're okay?" Veronica folds her arms

on the back of the seat and rests her chin on them.

"Leave her alone, Ronnie," Levi says from behind me.

"Fine," I say. "Just tired."

I tuck my hair behind my ear and look out the window, inwardly cursing myself because Josephine doesn't tuck her hair, she twirls it. I play with the ends and wrap the strands around my finger.

While we taxi out to the runway, I keep my eyes fixed on all the things going on outside. The other planes, the luggage carts moving around, the ground crew performing their various tasks. I'm too scared to look at Jarred sitting beside me for fear of him knowing I'm not his girlfriend. But how can he not tell something isn't right? Surely Josephine's friends have known her long enough to *know* her.

Shortly after take-off Jarred puts his hand on my knee. His touch makes me jump, and I turn to look at him.

He frowns. "What's up with you?"

I force a smile and try to relax, fitting my hand over his. "Nothing. I'm good."

Jarred leans towards me, and I think he's going to kiss me, but he nuzzles into my neck instead.

Shit.

I'm not prepared for how his warm breath on my skin makes me feel. My stomach flutters and I tense. I'm not supposed to react like this to my sister's boyfriend.

"We should relive Wednesday night when we get to my place," Jarred whispers in my ear.

Double shit!

Josephine must have given it up to Jarred this week. I can't believe she didn't tell me. No wonder Veronica

looked at me funny when she asked about Wednesday night, and Jarred had been giving me sideways glances. They have to know by now I'm not Josephine.

"Josie?" Jarred kisses my neck.

My throat is thick and I can't talk.

What the hell am I supposed to say?

Yes, I want to … Any girl in their right mind would want to be with Jarred.

I cross my legs because this is getting out of hand, and I want to jump on him right here on the plane.

But Josephine would never forgive me.

I would never forgive myself.

I lean into Jarred, hoping my body language tells him what he wants to hear, because I can't say anything.

And I can't say no. Josephine wouldn't say no.

But she told me to push him away.

The rest of the flight is torture. I look out the window as much as I can, avoiding Jarred's gaze. He keeps his hand on my knee, and as much as I like him touching me, I feel like I'm betraying my sister. Why did she want to do this? Is she testing me? Or testing Jarred? Whatever her reason is, I'm going to get it out of her tonight when we're both home.

We land and collect our luggage. No one is particularly talkative, for which I'm thankful, and we pile into the pre-booked bus transfer to go home. I sit up the back with Jarred and watch the city disappear behind us as we drive the highway north.

A few times I catch Jarred looking at me, and I'm not sure how to react. I've seen the way my sister is with him, and I do my best to smile and bat my lashes like she does, but his stare is burning me up inside.

Jarred leans towards me, my stomach flutters and my heart pounds. I lick my lips, sucking the bottom one between my teeth like I've seen Josephine do.

But he bypasses my mouth and whispers in my ear, "Nearly home."

His breath tickles the nape of my neck, and it's as if every hair on my body is standing on end. He slides his hand along my bare leg from my knee to my thigh.

Something hits Jarred in the cheek and I flinch.

"Wait until you're off the bus," Veronica says. "We don't want to see."

Jarred grabs the screwed-up boarding pass from the floor and chucks it back at her. "Jealousy doesn't look so good on you, Ronnie."

I glance at her, grateful she stopped me from doing something stupid, but what will I do when there's no one else around?

How the hell am I going to get out of this one?

I stop caring about anything

The airport shuttle bus pulls up outside Jarred's house and I follow him off. He grabs our luggage from the trailer. We wave goodbye to the others, and I look at my phone to check the time. It's quarter to five, which means Josephine and Stacey should be at least halfway home. If I hang around at Jarred's for too long, my sister will be home before me, and I'm not sure how well that will go down.

"I should get going soon." I follow Jarred up the path to his front door. The wheels on my case bump over the pebblecrete driveway as he pulls it along.

"We have time before my parents are home," Jarred says, stopping and pulling his house keys from his pocket. "Is there somewhere else you need to be?" He glances at me over his shoulder, a small smile playing on his lips,

before opening the door.

"No, of course not." I plaster my best Josephine smile on my face. "I just figure Mum and Dad will want to see me."

"They'll still be at work." Jarred sets our luggage in the foyer. "Like mine are." He raises his eyebrows and leans on the door, licking his lips.

My stomach tenses, and I struggle to keep my expression neutral.

What am I doing?

I step inside, trying not to be too obvious as I look around. I have only been in Jarred's house twice, so I'm not familiar with where everything is. Not familiar like Josephine should be. Jarred closes the front door and takes my hand, tugging me towards the huge staircase that sits to one side of the foyer.

My stomach twists into knots again, because upstairs means bedrooms. And a bedroom means ...

Just tell him.

I should tell Jarred what's going on. We're home now, and he doesn't seem to realise I'm Jessica, not Josephine. My sister has gotten what she wanted; to trick our friends. I need to end this now.

But I don't.

Instead, I put one foot on the bottom step, followed by another on the next step, and I let Jarred lead me to the upstairs level.

His house is the same as Veronica's in its grandeur, with lots of big rooms. I already know there's a tennis court and swimming pool out the back without having to look. My family is well off, but my parents are in no way pretentious or snobby. We live in a nice house, and

they drive nice cars. But we've never flaunted our wealth to the extent people do in Jarred's neighbourhood.

"You seem nervous." Jarred stops at the second door along the wide upstairs hallway. "It'll be even better this time, I promise." He leans down and kisses my neck.

My skin burns all over, and I take a sharp, shallow breath.

"I'm good," I manage to squeak out.

Jarred opens the door to what I assume is his room, and pulls me inside. The first thing I see is the queen-sized bed, and it seems so big. The door clicks closed behind me, and I jump.

Jarred frowns. "You don't want to do this?"

Oh god, yes. I want to do this.

I suck on my bottom lip. "I'm tired. Maybe we could … another time?"

Jarred lets go of my hand, and I let it fall to my side. His frown deepens as he studies me. The heat in his eyes makes me squirm. I twist my fingers together, and open my mouth to tell him I'm not who he thinks I am, but no words come out.

"You sure you're okay? You're acting a bit … like Jess."

"I'm fine," I lie. *Why did I lie?* He obviously knows something is wrong.

He steps towards me and touches my cheek with his fingers. I close my eyes, because looking at him is too hard.

Tell him.

I open my mouth again to speak and say he's right, I am Jessica, but I can't because Jarred's lips are on mine and his tongue is in my mouth. I squeeze my eyes closed tighter. I want to pull away, but all I can do is stand here and let him kiss me.

Then I'm kissing him back.

He has to know it's me and not Josephine.

His fingers press into my hips, pulling me closer to him.

A shiver runs through me, and my mind goes blank.

Jarred's hands move and lift the hem of my top.

What am I doing?

Josephine will kill me if she finds out.

How could I do this to her? To my sister?

"No," I mumble between our lips. "Stop." I push Jarred away and back up against the door. "We can't do this. I can't do this."

"Josie?" Jarred says, as if he's questioning whether I'm her or not. *I'm not!* Jarred draws in a long breath. He steps towards me and I have nowhere to go. "Tell me what's wrong," he continues. "You seemed pretty keen before we got to the airport."

My breaths are coming short and fast, and I try to slow them down, but I can't. How can he not realise he's kissing his girlfriend's sister? He *must* know.

What have I done?

Jarred closes the gap between us again, and I keep my eyes trained on his face, willing him to see that it's me and not Josephine.

"I'm ... I just can't do this ... with you," I whisper.

"Are you breaking up with me?"

Shit. "No ... I ..."

"But you don't want to be with me?"

My chest tightens again. "What are you going to do now that I've said no?"

"What? Nothing. I'm not *that* guy." Jarred shoves a

hand in his hair, then rubs his face before pressing both his palms to the door on either side of my head. "You were just so … keen. You've changed your mind?"

I nod.

Because I'm not your girlfriend, I yell at him in my head.

And then it hits me. Maybe Josephine wanted to swap because she doesn't want to be with Jarred. But why would she want that? What did he do to her? Did he hurt her?

"You know I love you," Jarred says. Then before I can reply, he leans in and kisses me again.

For the second time, I don't stop him.

This time it's different. Sweet. There's no pressure or force. Just his lips on mine, asking if it's okay.

I want it to be okay, but it isn't.

How can he not know?

Tears escape from the corners of my eyes, and my shoulders shake as I try to hold in a sob. Jarred pulls back, and I stare at our feet. His toes are touching mine.

"Why are you crying?" he asks.

"You don't feel it?"

"I'm feeling a lot of things."

I swipe my tears away, still staring at the floor. The door is hard against my back, and I concentrate on that before looking at Jarred again. When our eyes meet, I tuck my hair behind my ear, done with pretending to be someone I'm not.

"This isn't right," I say. "*Look* at me, Jarred."

I plead with my eyes for him to see me and not my sister. For him to not be just another guy who only sees his girlfriend as someone to have sex with.

Jarred takes a step back.

I wrap my arms around my middle.

"Fuck," Jarred says. "Jess? I knew it!"

I close my eyes and rest the back of my head against the door. "I'm sorry," I whisper.

"I knew there was something off about how you were acting. And the way you kissed me …" Jarred takes another step back, and another, until his legs hit the bed and he sits.

"I'm sorry," I say again.

A phone rings and it's not until I feel the vibration in my back pocket that I realise it's mine. I pull it out and stare at the screen, letting it ring.

"You going to get that?" Jarred asks.

I shake my head. "It's Josie. I can't talk to her right now."

Jarred puts his head in his hands. "Makes two of us," he mumbles.

My phone goes silent. A moment later a text comes through.

Josie: Where TF RU? I just got here. U should be home!

I chew my lip and hesitate before replying.

Me: Will B soon

"What does she want?"

"Probably to know if I've slept with you yet." I avoid Jarred's eyes.

He gets to his feet and paces the length of his large room, turning at his desk and walking back towards the bed. I press against the door, wishing I could go back to the moment I walked into the airport terminal, before any of this happened.

Do it all over again, only this time say no to my sister's dare.

Jarred paces a few more laps then stops in front of me, glaring at me.

"All we have to do is tell her nothing happened," I say.

He shakes his head. "It won't matter. She'll think the worst anyway." Jarred turns away from me and yells, throwing a punch at the wall that makes me flinch.

I've never seen him this angry.

He's scaring me.

"Can you take me home, please?" I say quietly.

Jarred nods and takes a deep breath, grabbing his keys from the desk. I follow him downstairs without a word, and he helps me get my luggage into his car. The drive home is uncomfortable, and twenty minutes feels like twenty hours. I hate myself for how good Jarred made me feel when he thought I was Josephine. Now, I don't know what to feel.

A few minutes from home I send Katie and Karen a text to let them know Stacey and I are home safe. Or at least I assume Stacey is, since my sister is waiting for me.

We pull up outside my house as the sky changes to the in between colour of dusk.

"You probably shouldn't come in," I say, fearing my sister and her boyfriend will fly off the handle at each other, and Josephine also at me. Even though this was her idea.

"Like hell." Jarred kills the engine and is out of the car before I can protest any further.

I sigh and get out as well, going around to the boot to get my bags. Despite Jarred being pissed off, he's still a gentleman and pulls my suitcase while I carry my bag.

The front door flies open before we reach it, and Josephine

steps onto the welcome matt. She doesn't say anything, but the way her lips are pursed and her brow is pinched shows she's obviously mad.

Well, I'm angry, too.

She should never have put me in this position.

"What the hell is wrong with you?" Jarred yells. He lets go of the handle on my suitcase, causing it to topple over.

"What did you do with her?" Josephine fires back.

"Nothing, but I know you won't believe that." Jarred clenches his fists.

I stand back and wait, because what am I supposed to say? I told you so? That's not going to fix this.

Josephine clenches her jaw and folds her arms. "You should've known it wasn't me."

Jarred shakes his head, and puts his hands on his hips. "Why the fuck did you do this, Josie?"

"Did you sleep with her?" She steps forward, asking the question as if I'm not even here.

Jarred draws in a long, deep breath, then lets it out. "No. I did not sleep with Jess."

I close my eyes and wish I could fly away from this, and whatever is going on between them. There is obviously something wrong. I blink a few times and wait, because I still don't know what to say.

"I don't believe you." Josephine hugs her stomach and screws up her face.

"See, that's the problem," Jarred says. "You're never going to believe me because you don't trust me."

"Can you blame me?" Josephine spits.

"Please, stop," I say, but neither of them acknowledge me.

"I don't need this shit." Jarred turns and walks back towards his car. "We're done," he calls over his shoulder.

Oh no. He's breaking up with her.

"What?" Josephine screams.

She steps forward and I grab her wrist. "Let him go. You both need time to cool off."

My sister spins to face me. "I don't need to cool off. I need to give him a piece of my mind. He can't break up with me."

"Would you listen to yourself?" I say, trying not to shout. "He's pissed at you because of this stunt we pulled. If I was him, I'd break up with you, too."

Jarred's car roars to life. The tyres squeal as he speeds away from the kerb.

Josephine's mouth forms an *O* and she glares at me. "You did sleep with him."

"No, I didn't." I grit my teeth. "He wanted to but—"

"But what?"

"I pushed him away … like you said." Tears sting my eyes and I bite my tongue to hold them back. But I can't. They spill onto my cheeks, and a sob bursts from my mouth.

"If nothing happened, why are you crying?"

Josephine stands with her hands on her hips. The sky is darker now, and a chill runs over my skin.

"He thought I was you," I say.

"Oh my God, Jessica, what happened," Josephine yells.

I shake my head. "If you hadn't dared me to swap with you, none of this would've happened. Jarred wouldn't have—"

"What? Tell me!"

I step back, because I know my sister loves me, but she's angry. "He kissed me … and I didn't stop him."

Air puffs from Josephine's mouth. "How could you?"

"How could I? How could *you* put me in this position?" I yell. "You're just as much of a bitch as Veronica."

The words are out of my mouth before I can take them back.

"You think I'm a bitch?"

"No, I—"

"Of all the people in my life, Jess, I never thought I'd hear you say that word to my face."

"I'm sorry," I say.

"For calling me a bitch or kissing my boyfriend?"

What I've done to my sister is wrong, and I desperately want to take it back, but what she did to me is wrong, too. I briefly wonder if I look like Josephine when I'm mad. Since we have the same face, I guess I do.

"I can't believe you did this to me," she yells again. "I'm your sister, Jess."

"Josie, it just happened, I'm sorry."

"It just happened! Oh my God, Jessica. Something like that does not *just happen.*"

I don't reply. What can I say to change things? Nothing is going to take back the fact I kissed Jarred.

And I liked it.

Josephine ducks inside and grabs her car keys from the bowl on the bookshelf near the front door.

"I'm going out," she says through gritted teeth.

"Where?" I follow her to her car. "Don't go after him, Josie. He's not worth it. No guy is worth coming between us."

Josephine spins to face me. "Right now, I'm mad at you. So just … let me go."

My sister gets into her car and slams the door. She shouldn't be driving when she's so angry. I want to stop her and make her see how stupid all of this is, but the car rumbles to life and she backs out of the driveway. I walk to the street as she tears off down the road. The way she floors it makes me worry, but I can't go after her now. I don't have my own car yet, and Mum and Dad aren't home.

Generally I'm considered the quiet twin. I've been labelled the 'nice' one while Josephine is the rebel. I've gotten pretty good at not letting my true feelings show, because Josephine is the highly-strung, emotional one, and does enough of it for both of us.

Fresh tears fall from my eyes, and I put my face in my hands, not even trying to hold them back.

"Jess?" a voice calls.

I raise my head and see Daniel Sullivan, Katie's brother, standing at the top of his driveway a few houses up the street. He waves, and I give a small wave back.

Daniel walks towards me, smiling, but his smile falters when he reaches me.

"Hey, Daniel, what's up?" I try to act normal.

"Are you okay?" He frowns. "You've been crying?"

We've grown up together, and Daniel sometimes knows me better than I know myself. There's no way I can get out of giving him a reason for why I'm crying, especially since it doesn't happen very often.

"I had a fight with Josie."

"She took off in a bit of a hurry." Daniel glances up

the street as if Josephine will appear again, coming back from wherever she stormed off to.

"She's a bit upset."

"Why, Jess? What happened?" He studies my face. "It must be bad."

"It's nothing." I swipe at my eyes then take a deep breath. "I should go after her."

Daniel glances towards his house. "I'll take you. We can use Mum's car. You can tell me what happened while we drive."

"I really don't want to talk about it," I say.

Daniel shrugs. "Okay."

It's one of the things I love about him. He's never pushy about anything. I've liked him for a really long time, and if he wasn't the brother of one of my closest friends, I would have hinted for him to ask me out ages ago. But I'm not sure how Katie would feel if Daniel and I got together.

"I'll lock up." I run back to the front door and rummage through Josephine's bag to find my house keys.

After checking my phone is still in my back pocket, I lock the house and make my way back to Daniel who is dawdling along the street towards his driveway.

"Any idea where Josie went?" Daniel asks as we get into the car.

"Jarred's place."

"That's a good thing, right?" Daniel turns the key and the engine rumbles to life.

"Well … he broke up with her, so I'm not sure."

"Oh." Daniel reverses onto the road.

I glance over to Levi's yard. No cars in the driveway,

so he must have gone out as soon as he got back. He's never been the kind of guy to stay home on a Friday night.

"Have you spoken to Katie?" I stare at Daniel as he drives up the road.

"She'll be home tomorrow. I can't wait to hear all about the week you girls had." He winks at me, making my stomach flip.

My cheeks heat and I look away. "I'll direct you to Jarred's once we get to the end of the freeway."

The night is cloudy and our street is dark, the moon hiding like I want to. Everything lights up when we reach the main road that runs through our suburb. The noise of people talking in the local shops, grabbing take-away or last-minute groceries, drifts through my open window. We leave it all behind when we turn left at the roundabout.

"I like the back way to the highway," Daniel says. "Less traffic."

We go down the hill, and as we come back up over the rise, flashing red and blue lights illuminate the horizon.

"Looks like an accident or something," I say.

As we draw closer, I get a better picture of what's going on. There's a car up on the kerb, the driver's side wrapped around the telegraph pole on the corner. Another car sits in the intersection, the front smashed.

"We're not going to get through." Daniel turns right into a random driveway.

"I hope everyone is okay." I stare out the window as Daniel puts the car in reverse.

I squint through the darkness at the car on the corner. A tarpaulin covers the driver's side of the front windscreen, taped up as a makeshift veil.

The lights flash. I make out the dark colour of the small car, and the silver H for Honda on the grille. Then I see the letters of the numberplate.

"Josie?" Her name puffs from my mouth. Daniel reverses onto the road. "Stop!" I yell, flinging the door open before he can ask why. I tumble out of the car while it's still moving, falling onto the road and scraping my hands. "No. No, NO!" I scramble to my feet and run towards the wreck on the corner.

Towards Josephine's smashed car.

Daniel's voice floats behind me, but I'm not listening. I have to get to my sister. There are people on the scene, but I race past them to the passenger side of Josephine's car.

"You can't be here," someone yells as I rip the door open.

Josephine is limp in the driver's seat, her seatbelt holding her in place. The side of her face looks black under the streetlight. Lines of blood have run into her eyes from a huge gash on her forehead. Droplets of red have collected on the ends of her eyelashes like little glass beads.

A whimper escapes my mouth, and I climb into the passenger seat on my knees as someone tries to grab me. I kick out and scream, "No!" I make it to my sister, and attempt to shake her awake.

"You need to get back, Miss." Hands reach into the car and grab my shoulders, and this time I feel too weak to fight them. I let them pull me out of the car.

"Josie!" I sob. "No. You can't do this. You can't die. Please, please. I'm so sorry. Josie ..."

"Sister," I hear Daniel say, and then his arms are around me.

"We're trying to get hold of her parents," another voice says. "The other driver survived, but has been taken to hospital in critical condition."

I sob into Daniel's chest.

My sister is gone.

"Can you tell us the other driver's name?" Daniel asks.

I don't care who it is.

In this moment I stop caring about anything.

Promise

aniel leads me away from Josephine's smashed car.

I'm not sure how I'm walking. My legs are weak, and they buckle at the knees. Daniel catches me and lets me down gently onto the footpath, sitting beside me.

Red and blue lights flash.

A siren sounds.

I stare up the street at the people coming out of their houses, and I want to scream at them to go away.

Josephine's bloody face fills my mind, and I tangle my fingers into my hair, trying to pull the image out of my head so I don't have to look at it.

"She's dead," I breathe. "Nooooo. She can't be dead. This is my fault. All my fault."

"It's not your fault," Daniel whispers in my ear, rubbing my back.

I pull my knees to my chest and bury my face in them, hugging myself tight so I don't fall apart.

"Excuse me, Miss?" a voice says. Then a hand is on my shoulder.

I look up at a police officer. She has a kind face, but she can't hide the shine of tears in her eyes.

I wipe my nose with the back of my hand and tuck my hair behind my ears. "Yes?"

She crouches in front of me. "I'm Officer Brinley. What's your name?"

"Jessica." I stare at her. "Jessica Hart."

She presses her lips together into a thin line. "Is that your sister in the car?"

I nod as my throat thickens, and I choke on the word, "Yes." I squeeze my eyes closed but there are too many tears to hold in, and they spill out like a dam bursting. My chest aches as I put my face in my hands and sob.

"How did this happen?" Daniel asks.

"We're trying to figure that out," Officer Brinley says. "We also need to reach your parents." She touches my arm again. "Are they at home?"

"They weren't when I left," I say through my hands.

"Is there a number I might be able to reach them on?" Officer Brinley asks softly.

A painful lump has formed in my throat, and I can't speak. With shaky hands I fumble my phone from my back pocket and drop it. Daniel retrieves it from the ground at my feet and hands it back to me. I put in my pass code, bringing up Mum's mobile number on the screen. Officer Brinley writes it down.

"I'll try this. See if I can reach either of them," she

says. "I'll also send an officer over to your house."

"Can you tell us who was driving the other car?" Daniel asks. "I have a friend who drives a BMW."

My skin turns to ice as I break out in a sweat.

The other car is a BMW?

"I'm not supposed to release any information," Officer Brinley says.

Daniel gets to his feet, as does the officer. I stare up at them both.

"Please," Daniel says.

Officer Brinley presses her lips together again. "Levi White. I'll make this call. See if I can contact Jessica's parents."

The air is sucked from my lungs as if I've been punched in the gut.

"Levi?" I stare at Daniel.

He sits back beside me and pulls me into his arms. The tears come faster, and I can't stop the shakes that rack my body.

"Katie," I say. "On no. Nooooo," I wail into Daniel's chest. "My fault. My fault."

"Stop saying that, Jess." Daniel hugs me tighter, and I struggle in his embrace.

He's suffocating me.

I can't breathe.

But Daniel doesn't let go. He whispers in my ear, telling me everything will be okay. But how can that be true? My sister is dead. I've lost the other side of me. The part that has always made me feel whole. Now what am I? Just half a person?

What will I do without her?

How do I survive without Josephine?

I curl into Daniel, staring at the accident scene I can't seem to look away from. If I close my eyes all I see is Josephine, trapped in the driver's seat of her car. I watch as they pull the Honda away from the telegraph pole, and mark the ground with spray paint. They've put up road blocks so no one can get through the intersection. Quite a few people are on the street watching now, as if it's some great new TV show everyone has to see.

A car pulls up behind Daniel's. A police cruiser also stops but doesn't bother pulling over. It sits in the middle of the road with its lights flashing. A woman gets out of the first car and races towards us. She's frantic, and it's not until she's a couple of metres away that I see Mum's contorted face. Dad is close behind.

"My baby girl, where is she?" Mum runs right past us.

"Ma'am, please wait," calls an officer from the new police car on the scene.

Officer Brinley intercepts Mum before she can get too close to the wreck. Dad is at her side, and neither of them has seen me.

"We'll need you to stay back. You can see her later, once she's freed from the wreckage and the coroner has taken a look," Officer Brinley says as the new police officer joins them.

I untangle myself from Daniel and stand on wobbly legs. He takes my elbow but I gently pull away and walk towards my parents.

"Mum?" I say when I reach them.

She turns and looks at me, and for a moment it's as if she doesn't know who I am.

Her face crumples, and she pulls me into her arms. Dad wraps us both up in his embrace, and my mum and I cry together, our sobs echoing each other's. Mum mumbles words through her tears, but I can't understand them. I don't speak. My heart hurts.

Everything hurts.

Dad lets go of us, and I pull back from Mum to see why. He's watching the commotion, and I stare as two ambulance officers take a stretcher out and extend the legs, wheeling it over to Josephine's car.

"Maybe you should go home and get some rest," Officer Brinley says, touching Dad's arm. "We can call you tomorrow to sort everything out."

"We can't leave our baby girl," Mum says through her tears.

Dad puts an arm around her shoulders. "We want to stay."

"I understand that," the officer says, "but there is really nothing you can do here. I'm sorry for your loss, but the best thing now is to let us look after Josephine. She's in good hands, I promise." Officer Brinley smiles, and I fix my gaze on the shadows dancing across her face, cast by the strobing red and blue lights.

Dad nods. "We'll wait for a call tomorrow."

"I'll personally contact you," Officer Brinley says.

I hug myself and rub my arms, attempting to ward away the chill that has crept under my skin. Daniel puts a hand on my shoulder. This time I don't try to shrug him off. I lean into him, and let him hug me.

"Daniel? What are you doing here?" Dad asks. But before he can answer, Dad turns his stare to me. "Jess?

Do you know what happened?"

"I ..." I put a hand to my mouth and stifle a sob, shaking my head. "We had a fight. Josie left so I asked Daniel to ... We followed her and found her ..." I squeeze my eyes closed and turn my face into Daniel's chest.

"Let's get home," Dad says.

Daniel walks me to our car and helps me into the back seat. "I'll come and see you tomorrow."

When he closes the door, it's as if he's a million miles away, and I feel so alone. I glance over to the empty seat beside me, and the realisation that Josephine will never sit there again hits me.

Mum sobs quietly in the front passenger seat. Dad starts the car and does a U-turn in the street, heading towards our house. I look out the back window at Daniel standing on the footpath, the red and blue lights of the ambulance and police sirens flashing behind him.

I rest my head against the cool glass of the window and close my eyes. A few minutes later, Dad pulls into our driveway. He gets out and helps Mum from the car. I have no energy. All I want to do is stay where I am, and concentrate on the cold sensation on my cheek.

If I stay like this I won't have to feel anything else.

If I go inside the house there will be too many things that remind me of Josephine.

The car door opens and I jolt, losing the cool patch from the glass. I rub my cheek, and Dad reaches down to take my arm. He helps me into the house, and as I walk along the path to the front door, I think about all the things I will do from now on that I won't get to do with my sister.

All the things she will never do with me.

We will never see another movie together, or go shopping together.

We will never argue over who has to unpack the dishwasher, or whose turn it is to sweep the driveway.

We will never make popcorn and talk, like we had planned to tonight.

I will never get to hug her again.

My thoughts are too much, and a fresh wave of tears hits me as we step into the foyer and Dad closes the front door.

"I think I'll go to bed," I say. "Maybe tomorrow I'll wake up and this nightmare will be over."

Dad's eyes shine bright with tears. "Okay, sweetie."

He leads me to the stairs, and I catch my reflection in the mirror above the low bookshelf near the front door. One thing I *will* get to do is look at Josephine every day. Because she is me and I am her.

We are two pieces of one whole. A whole that is now broken.

Mum follows us as Dad helps me downstairs to my room. No one says anything, and the air is filled with the soft sniffles and short breaths of grief. How are we going to make it through this?

I crawl under the blankets on my bed, and bury my face in my pillow.

"I've been waiting to see you so I could ask how your week was." Mum sits on the edge of my bed and strokes my hair.

I roll my head to the side and stare at my parents. They must hate that I look exactly like their dead daughter.

"None of it matters now." I squeeze my eyes closed, and let out a soul-shattering sob. "Why? Why Josie? Why, why, why?"

Mum and Dad cover me with their arms, hugging me through the blankets.

"We don't know, sweetie," Mum whispers. "We don't know."

I lie with what's left of my family, listening to their breathing, comforted by the weight of their embrace.

Mum continues to stroke my hair, and after a while she says, "Try to get some sleep."

Dad rubs my back. "We'll be upstairs if you need us."

All I do is nod, because I don't plan on getting out of bed any time soon.

Maybe never.

My parents leave, switching off my bedroom light on their way out and leaving the door ajar. The switch clicks in the hallway as Mum flicks the light on. A yellow glow spills into my room, casting a triangle onto the floor.

I curl into the foetal position and hug my knees. If I stay right where I am I won't have to face anything. I won't have to look at myself. At my dead sister who will always be alive in my face. I won't ever be able to look in a mirror and see myself. I will always see her.

My phone buzzes in my back pocket, and I realise that I haven't even changed yet. I'm still wearing Josephine's clothes, and she was wearing mine when she died. The thought brings on a fresh flood of tears, and when I finally manage to get my phone out and look at it, the screen is a blur.

I blink a few times to refocus so I can read the text

message.

Daniel: I won't ask if UR OK. Want me 2 come over?

The words on the screen torment me. I want to be alone right now, but I also need someone to hold me together, because I don't know if I can do it myself.

Me: Laundry door

Daniel: B 5 mins

I lie in bed clutching my phone until I hear Daniel's footsteps outside my bedroom window. With a heavy heart I push myself to sitting and set my feet onto the floor. My legs are weak, and the short walk down the hallway to the laundry at the end of the house is exhausting.

I've never felt so tired in my life.

When I open the back door, Daniel is leaning against the brick wall, the outside sensor light making his auburn hair gleam. My heart skips, then I frown because I shouldn't be thinking about how hot my neighbour is when my sister just died.

Daniel looks down at me. "I wanted to make sure ..." He shrugs. "You know."

"Thank you." I chew the inside of my cheek and stare at my feet.

"Can I come in?"

Without answering, I step back and let Daniel into the laundry. He follows me to my room, and I climb under the blankets again. He sits in the chair at my desk.

"Do you want to talk? Or just ... I can ..." He shrugs again. "I can just sit with you?"

"Either would be nice." I pull the blankets up to my chin, and get comfortable on my side so I can see his face. He sits with his hands in his lap, looking down at

them and pressing his fingertips together.

"People are going to say a lot of stuff to you over the next few days." He twists from side to side in the chair. "Weeks and months even. They'll look at you with pity for a really long time."

Daniel goes quiet, and I wait for him to keep talking because I like the sound of his voice. It doesn't matter what he's saying, it only matters that he cares enough to say it in the first place.

"Everyone will ask if you're okay, and they'll want to hug you." He takes a deep breath. "But you have to know that it's all right to *not* be okay. I wasn't after ..."

"Mason," I whisper.

He nods. "But enough about that, we were talking about you."

"No, it's okay. I miss Mason sometimes, too."

Daniel losing Mason might not be exactly the same as me losing Josephine, but when his best friend, Levi's brother, died, I know Daniel felt like he'd lost his real brother.

We all felt like we'd lost a part of ourselves.

I smile at the thought of Mason, because remembering that Levi, and the rest of us, got through it, gives me hope. Then I frown again, because Levi is the one who hit Josephine's car, and he's in the hospital.

I'm not sure how I'm supposed to feel about that.

Should I hate him? Or should I be upset that he's really hurt?

Do I have enough tears for my sister *and* Levi?

"Does Katie know what's happened?" I ask. "She's going to be ..."

Daniel looks up from his hands. "Yeah, she's going to … We haven't called her. Mum and Dad think it's best not to tell Katie and Karen until they get home tomorrow. We want them to drive safely. They might not do that if they know what's happened."

"Have you … heard anything about Levi?" I ask.

Daniel runs a hand through his hair and sits forward, leaning his elbows on his knees. "He's not good. Coma."

I blow a breath out between my lips and turn my face into my pillow, pulling my arms up over my head. My eyes are burning from crying so much, but I can't stop the tears that come again. Everything hurts, and I want to fall asleep so I don't have to feel the pain.

I sense Daniel has moved closer, and then his hand is on my shoulder. When I peek out from under my arm, he is kneeling on the floor beside my bed. The weight of his hand on me is comforting, but if he knew why Josephine died, and that it was my fault, he probably wouldn't be here.

I want to tell him what happened.

I want to tell him about Jarred, but I also don't want him to go away.

What would he say if he knew what I did to my sister?

I rub my face, and tuck my hair behind my ear. "There's something you should know."

Daniel moves his hand to my cheek, caressing my skin with his thumb. "You don't have to talk about anything tonight, Jess."

"It's my fault," I say before I chicken out. "I did something that made Josie *really* mad. And she had that accident. I should've tried harder to stop her leaving."

Daniel shakes his head. "No. It's not your fault. You weren't driving."

"But *she* was driving because of *me*."

My shoulders shake as I cry harder. Hot tears pour down my cheeks and burn my skin like lava.

"Shh," Daniel says. His hands are now in my hair, and he presses his forehead to mine. "I'm going to help you get through this. You're not alone. Okay?"

I grip his wrist and nod, then let him pull me into his arms. We sit like that for a while, Daniel kneeling on my bedroom floor holding my tired body and broken heart. He makes me feel safe, and I wish we could stay like this forever.

But tomorrow will come, and my sister will still be dead.

I must have nodded off, because when I jolt awake my head is on my pillow and Daniel's arms are no longer around me. My heart races as my eyes adjust to the gloom. I can't see him, and I suddenly feel so alone.

"Daniel?" I sit up. "Where are you?"

"Jess, I'm here. It's okay." He scoots forward on my desk chair, emerging from the shadows, the dull moonlight illuminating one side of his face. My bedroom door is closed, a thin line of light from the hallway seeps under the bottom. Daniel must have closed it when I fell asleep.

"I thought you left," I say.

"I didn't want you to freak out if you woke up and I wasn't here."

"I freaked out anyway."

"Sorry I made you feel that way." He smiles and slips his hand into mine.

I settle under my blankets again, still gripping Daniel's

hand, and close my eyes. The weight of his palm touching mine anchors me, helping me avoid the images of Josephine that linger at the edges of my mind.

"Will you be here tomorrow?" I whisper.

Daniel runs circles over the back of my hand with his thumb, making my skin tingle. "I will be here whenever you need me."

"I miss her."

"I know."

Tears squeeze from the corners of my tightly closed eyes. "Will you stay while I fall asleep again?"

"I'm not going anywhere."

"Promise?" I ask, my eyes still shut.

"Promise."

Come back

Sunlight streams through my window and I blink against the glare. I grab my phone from my bedside table to see the time. It's almost eleven o'clock, and I wonder why Mum hasn't come to wake me yet. She never lets me and Josephine sleep in past ten.

Then memories of last night come flooding back.

Josephine dead in her car.

All the tears I cried.

Daniel holding my hand while I fell asleep.

Daniel. He must have gone home.

I sit up in bed, a feeling of pure emptiness settling in my stomach. There's a note on my bedside table. I pick it up and unfold it.

> *I didn't want your parents to find me in your
> room. I'll come by before lunch. Daniel x*

I run my finger over the X he left after his name, and smile. But I shouldn't be smiling. I shouldn't be feeling all warm and fuzzy because of a kiss a guy left me on a piece of paper. Not when my sister isn't here to share it with.

Footsteps sound on the stairs. A few moments later there's a knock on my door. I lean back against the bedhead and take a deep breath.

"Jess?" Mum says. "Are you awake?"

"Sure, Mum. Come in."

My door opens slowly and Mum looks down at me, her eyes puffy and rimmed with red. She takes a couple of steps into my room then stops, pressing her lips together.

"Sleep okay?" she asks, wringing her hands.

I nod but don't say anything. I can't tell her the only reason I could sleep was because Daniel had been here with me. She probably wouldn't mind that I had a boy in my room, but she would care that I hadn't asked her to stay instead.

"Want some help choosing something to wear today?" She picks up a jumper I must have left on the floor before I went away and folds it, setting it on the seat of my chair.

I shake my head. "I want to try to get more sleep."

"Whatever you need, sweetie. But I think you should come and eat something first."

My mother is the nicest person I know. She always has something positive to say, and I can't remember the last time I heard her yell. She's beautiful, and kind. Her eyes are the same clear blue as mine, but her hair is a deep chocolate, the result of grey-covering dye jobs.

I like to think I'm like Mum. Sometimes I wonder where Josephine got her wild streak from. We are—were—so

different. Thoughts of my sister creep into my mind, thoughts I've been trying so hard to keep at bay, and my eyes sting.

"I'm not hungry. I want to sleep forever," I whisper, lying down and pulling my blankets up.

"Oh, Jess." Mum puts a hand to her mouth. "Please don't say that."

The pain in her eyes makes me wish I'd never said those words, but I still feel them. I squeeze my eyes closed and burrow into my pillow. I shouldn't be shutting Mum out, but I can't help it. If she knew what I did to Josephine, she'd hate me.

The bed dips with Mum's weight as she sits on the edge. "You might feel better if you have a shower. Your dad and I ... We have to go and see Josie. Sort out some things. Do you want to come?"

My chest aches at the thought of seeing my dead sister. I shake my head and sob, unable to lift my head and look at Mum.

She rubs my arm through the blankets. "Okay. We'll be back this afternoon. Try to eat something before we get home. I'll leave some fruit on the bench."

Her weight leaves the bed, and I peek out of my blanket cave as she disappears into the hallway. She sets the door slightly open the way she always does. I lie and listen to my parents as they move around upstairs. Knuckles rap on the front door, and hurried footsteps sound overhead. I snuggle under my blankets, resigning myself to a day, probably longer, of more crying.

I don't want to face the world. I don't want to face anyone.

The front door creaks, and Mum says, "Daniel, please come in. She's in her room."

"Thanks, Bridget," Daniel replies, and the sound of his voice calms me a little.

"Ready to go?" I hear Dad ask, and imagine him standing beside Mum at the door as Daniel tries to squeeze past.

"Try to get her out of bed, please?" Mum says, and I cringe.

The front door closes. Footsteps sound on the stairs again.

"Knock, knock," Daniel says from the hallway. "Jess?"

"Come in." I fold the blanket away from my face, and brush my hair back with one hand.

Daniel pushes the door open and stands in the middle of my room, his hands in his pockets. I try to smile, but all I want to do is cry again. I never thought I'd have so many tears. They should have dried up by now, I've cried so many.

"How are you feeling today?" Daniel asks.

"Like my sister just died." The words are out before I can stop them. I don't want to be that girl. The one who's a bitch when someone is trying to help me. "Sorry. I didn't mean it to sound so ..."

"It's okay." Daniel moves my jumper from the chair and sits down. "Have you had a shower? They usually make me feel better."

"You sound like my mum."

"Or sunlight," Daniel says. "We could go and sit outside?"

I shake my head. "I want to stay here."

"Okay. How about I get you a drink of water and

something to eat? I bet you haven't had breakfast, and it's almost lunch time."

"Mum said she'd leave fruit on the bench."

"Perfect." Daniel stands and leaves the room.

While he's gone, I realise I haven't gotten up since Mum and Dad put me in bed last night, and I need to pee. Once I start thinking about it, the urge gets stronger, and I jump out of bed and run to the bathroom.

I wash my hands, and catch a glimpse of my reflection in the mirror. My heart pounds and my palms go sweaty. The face staring back at me doesn't feel like my own anymore.

It's the face of a ghost.

Mascara has run under my eyes. Makeup that Josephine applied at the airport to make me more like her. All I can do is stare as the me in the mirror cries and cries, wishing Josephine was standing here in my place. Wishing I could tell her I love her. Wishing that the last time I saw her alive we hadn't been fighting, but laughing instead.

"It's not fair!" I scream at the mirror. "I hate you. I hate you!"

My fingers ache from clenching my fists. I push my palms against the glass panel in front of me, dragging my nails down the slick surface, trying to hurt the person in the reflection. It's her fault. All her fault.

"Jess?" Daniel says from the other side of the door.

I don't answer.

I can't.

All I can do is sob. I raise one hand and slap the mirror, letting out a scream. The contact makes my hand sting.

"Jess!" Daniel says my name again, his voice more

frantic. "Answer me or I'm coming in.

Slap.

I scream again.

The bathroom door flies open. "Hey, Jess. Stop." Daniel grabs my wrists, hugging me from behind, and crosses my arms over my chest. "You'll hurt yourself."

I press my back against him and go limp. "It already hurts."

"I know," he whispers. "Just breathe."

"How do I do that? I feel like I'm drowning and I can't make it to the surface."

"Let's get you back to your room."

Daniel helps me along the hallway. When I walk through the door to my bedroom, I see myself in the full-length mirror on the front of my wardrobe. My breath hitches, and my heart aches, because I look exactly like Josephine from head to toe.

I'm still wearing my sister's clothes, and it's as if she is there in the mirror, trapped in another world, desperate to escape.

"She loved these denim shorts," I say. "And this top. It was her favourite shade of green."

I rub the fabric between my fingers, and suddenly, I feel dirty. I'm not worthy to be wearing something my sister has worn so many times. I betrayed her. I'm not worthy of anything.

I open my mouth and let out a gut-wrenching cry, then run at the mirror with my hands up. I can't look at my refection anymore. The mirror has to go, and if I have to rip it down with my bare hands, I will.

"Go away!" I yell at my reflection. "Leave me alone."

"Jess. Jess, stop." Daniel grabs at my arms, but I push him away.

"Stop looking at me," I scream at the mirror, raising my fists.

"Jessica!" Daniel grabs me from behind again, locking my arms to my sides in a strong hug. "You'll hurt yourself."

I'll hurt myself? Everything already hurts. I've already hurt my sister. I struggle against Daniel, trying to get at the girl in the mirror so I can make her go away.

I need her to go away.

"I'm not letting go until you calm down," Daniel says, his voice soft near my ear.

"I can't look at her. I can't. It's my fault. She has to go. She's everywhere I look. Make her go away. She has to go away. My fault."

"None of this is your fault."

I stop fighting, exhaustion settling into my bones.

Daniel leads me to the bed and pulls the covers back. "You need to rest."

I drop onto the edge of the bed, and stare at a spot on the floor. "I *need* to get these clothes off. They ... They're Josie's."

Daniel stands in front of me, his feet blocking the spot on the floor I'm studying. I look over at the mirror. My face, Josephine's face, is drawn and tired. Red-rimmed eyes and stringy hair. Daniel crouches in front of me, putting a hand on my cheek and turning my head so I'm looking at him.

"Want me to cover it up?" he asks.

I nod. Daniel takes a throw rug from the blanket box at the end of my bed, opens my wardrobe door and hangs

the rug over the top so it covers most of the mirror. He closes the door again to keep the rug from falling off.

"Can you change on your own?" he asks.

My face heats, but I'm too tired and too upset to be embarrassed. I shrug, because my body has gone numb, and I don't want to move.

Daniel looks around the room. "Wardrobe or drawers?"

"I have tops in the second drawer, and shorts in the third." I point to the dresser, then stare at the floor again.

Daniel fumbles through my clothes, choosing a pale yellow singlet top and a pair of black and white shorts. "These do?"

I nod, because I don't care what I look like.

"Um ..." He glances at the dresser again then back at me. "Do you want fresh underwear?"

"That would be nice. Top left."

Daniel opens the drawer and looks into it. "Um ..."

"Have you never seen Katie's underwear?" I smile, but it feels wrong on my face. I shouldn't be smiling.

"She's my sister. I don't make a habit of looking in her drawers." Daniel turns to face me. "And she usually has clothes on when I see her."

My smile widens, because he's clearly uncomfortable, and I should put him out of his misery.

"You have a beautiful smile," Daniel says.

A breath puffs out between my lips. "Thanks."

I tuck my hair behind my ears and look away, getting to my feet and taking the few steps across the room to my dresser. I grab a fresh pair of knickers and a bra before closing the drawer.

"I'll um ..." Daniel hands me my top and shorts, then

opens the door. "... just be in the hallway."

After he closes the door I strip off and change, tossing my underwear into the hamper in the corner, and folding Josephine's clothes before putting them on the lid. For some reason I can't explain, I don't want to put them in the dark hamper with my dirty clothes.

"I'm done," I say, opening the door.

"Feel better?"

"Not really." I hug myself, and sit on the edge of the bed. "I want to go to sleep. I'm really tired."

"Okay. But you should eat first." Daniel points to my side table. "I made you some toast. And there's fruit."

There's a glass of water sitting beside the plate. I pick it up and take a couple of sips before setting it back down. The thought of eating makes my stomach clench, but I put a few grapes in my mouth, and nibble at the piece of toast anyway.

"Thanks." I put the half-eaten slice back on the plate.

"Want me to stay?" Daniel asks.

I nod as my throat tightens. The threat of more tears looms, and I wish I could stop them, but fighting them makes me exhausted. Daniel sits in my desk chair, and I climb into bed.

He doesn't talk. He just sits with me. My phone rings on my side table, and I read Veronica's name on the screen. I shake my head. Daniel reaches over and hits the red hang-up button. I close my eyes, but sleep doesn't come easily, although I must drift a little because the next thing I hear is a whispering voice.

"I think she's sleeping," Daniel says.

I open my eyes to slits and I'm staring at the wall. I

must have rolled over in my sleep. The bed dips with the weight of someone sitting on it, but I don't open my eyes fully because if I keep them closed I won't have to face whoever it is.

"How's she doing?" I hear Katie's voice.

"Not so good," Daniel replies.

"What are you …" Katie takes a breath. "You and …?"

"You weren't here." Daniel says. "She needed someone."

There's a moment of silence, and I strain my ears, trying to hear if they're whispering more quietly.

"Is there …?" Katie seems like she wants to ask Daniel if there's anything going on between us. I don't blame her. It probably looks a little odd, finding her brother in my room.

"Katie, I'm just trying to help."

"Why didn't you call me?" she asks.

"We wanted you and Karen to get home safely," Daniel says. "We didn't want you both worrying, and rushing to get back here. We can talk more when you get home."

"See you soon," Katie says.

"I'll take you to the hospital later if you like."

The hospital … Levi. Katie must be so upset about coming home to find out her boyfriend is in a coma. But at least he's not dead, like Josephine. I squeeze my eyes closed tighter, as if that will stop the pain from resurfacing.

"Maybe tomorrow," Katie says.

Daniel must be leaving. I don't want him to. I want him to stay. Was he only here because no one else was? I hope not. Despite thinking this, I don't speak up.

I hear the door close, and whoever is sitting on the bed sniffles. I assume it's Karen, because Katie and Karen

come as a package deal. Where's Stacey? I need my best friend, and I realise that I haven't even called her to tell her what's happened. Did she work out Josephine was pretending to be me? I've been so wrapped up in grief, I forgot to call her. Maybe Mum did.

The bed dips again, and someone lies down beside me with their stomach to my back. I finally open my eyes a little, and move so I can see my friends from the corner of my eye. Katie puts an arm over me and slips her hand into mine. I give it a squeeze.

"I'm so sorry," she whispers.

Both my friends hug me, and Katie plays with my hair. I blink a few times then close my eyes, hoping to keep the tears at bay, but I can't. One tear breaks free and slides down my cheek onto my nose. My breaths are shaky, and Katie and Karen hug me tighter.

The door creaks as someone else comes into the room. I smell Stacey's floral perfume before she climbs onto the bed, placing herself between me and the wall.

"Hey you," she says.

I swat the tears from my cheeks. "Hey."

Stacey twists the ends of my hair around her fingers, and the motion reminds me of how Josephine used to do the same thing with her golden strands.

Everything crashes down again.

"It's all my fault," I whisper.

"Oh no, Jess," Stacey says. "It's not your fault."

"Yes it is." I pull my pillow over my head and push my face into the mattress.

"It was an accident." Katie strokes my hair. "Just an accident."

"All my fault," I say again.

I scream into the mattress, over and over, clutching the sheets in my fists.

"It's okay," Stacey says. "Everything will be okay."

"Nooooo," I shout. "Nothing is okay. I did this. It's my fault. I did this, Josie. Oh my God, Josie!"

Katie gets up, and Stacey tries to hug me, but I push her away. They're suffocating me. Stacey and Karen get off the bed, too.

"It's not your fault, Jess," Katie says.

I look at her. Tears stain her cheeks.

"I killed her," I yell. "It's my fault ... all my fault."

"What do we do?" Karen whispers.

Stacey kneels beside the bed and whispers to me, "It's okay, you're okay. I'm here."

I push my face into my pillow again. "Josie. Josie, Josie, Josie."

"We're here for you," Katie says. "Always."

I turn my head and she's there, her head on the mattress beside mine. She smiles, and brushes my hair out of my eyes.

"Where's Josie?" I ask. *I want to see her.*

"Shh." Katie tucks my hair behind my ear.

"Josie," I say again.

"It's all right," Katie says. "Close your eyes."

"Can I see Josie?" I blink at her through a haze of tears.

"I'm sure you can see her any time you like," Katie says. "All you have to do is close your eyes."

"Josie, Josie, Josie, Josie, Josie." I repeat her name over and over, and close my eyes like Katie said to, hoping my sister will come back.

When she was alive

The past week has been the hardest of my life. Even harder than the night I found Josephine dead in her car, because now I know she definitely isn't coming back.

Mum and Dad have been racing around all over the place, busy with police reports and funeral arrangements. I don't want to get involved. Stuff like that is an adult's job. Besides, knowing the details will just make everything so much harder.

Every mirror in the house is now covered in some way. I can't bear to look at myself because I don't see me. I see the other side of me. The side that's not alive anymore. The side that died in that car with my sister.

I haven't been answering the phone or getting out of bed much, even when my friends come to see me. Veronica has been calling, but I don't want to talk to her. And I

haven't heard from Jarred. When he came to give his condolences, I told Mum I didn't want to see him. I can't face him after what happened between us.

Daniel has dropped in every day, and the only time I feel a bit better is when he's here. When I'm with him the weight I'm carrying seems lighter, but then he leaves and the emptiness creeps back in.

Today, I manage to have a shower and get dressed.

Small victories and all that.

Now, I'm sitting on my bed, staring out the window at the bush behind our house, feeling lost and not knowing what to do with myself. If Josephine was here, she'd drag me to the shops, or we'd spend some time planning the trip we wanted to take together before starting university.

A year off to travel.

We had such big dreams.

We wanted to buy round the world tickets. Take nothing but a backpack each. See as much as we could, with Rome and New York high on the list.

"Jess?" Mum's voice comes from the other side of my bedroom door.

"Come in."

The door swings open and Mum stops, leaning on the jamb and holding a shoebox. A plate with two slices of vegemite toast sits on top if it.

"How are you this morning?"

"Fine," I say, which is what I've been saying every morning, even though I'm far from fine. "What's with the box?"

Mum comes and sits beside me on the bed, resting the box on her knees. "Eat." She passes me the plate.

Her eyes are bright with tears, and she blinks a few times before using her finger to wipe at the corners.

"Thanks." I take the toast and nibble at it, waiting for her to tell me about the shoebox.

"The accident site …" Mum stops and presses her lips together. "People have been leaving things for Josie. I thought … We shouldn't leave them to get ruined by the weather, so …" She looks down at the box and takes a deep breath. "This is what I've collected so far. I thought it might help you if you read some of the notes and letters. There are photos in here, too."

I set my toast back on the plate and put it on my side table, staring at the box, unsure what to think or feel. What has everyone been writing and saying about Josephine? I haven't left the house, and the only people I've spoken to are Stacey, Karen, Katie, and Daniel. I touch the lid of the box, and Mum pushes it into my hands.

"I … I'm not sure I can look," I say.

"That's okay," she replies with a sad smile. "But it's here when you're ready. If you put it on your desk I'll add to it if anyone leaves something new at the site."

The box is heavy, as if it holds the weight of Josephine's entire life inside it. I stand and put it on my desk, pushing it to the wall, unable to look at the contents yet. Maybe in time I'll be able to, but not now.

"The funeral is tomorrow," Mum says.

"I know." *As if I'd forget.*

"Are you prepared?"

My chest tightens at the thought of giving Josephine's eulogy. "Yeah, Mum." *Will I ever be ready?*

"I'm sure whatever you say will be beautiful." Mum

smiles again. "I've been meaning to talk to you about something else. Your dad and I would like you to see someone. We've made an appointment with a psychologist."

I frown and sit on the bed again, leaning against the bedhead and crossing my legs. "Why? What for?"

Mum sighs. "We think you need some help."

"I'm fine," I whisper, looking at my fingers.

"Jess, sweetie. You're not." Mum puts a hand on my arm. "You won't even look at yourself in the mirror." She goes quiet, and I stare out the window. "I miss Josie, too," she continues. "But I miss you just as much. Talk to me. Tell me what's going on in that head of yours."

I keep my gaze fixed on the world outside my bedroom. "Really, Mum. I don't want to talk about it."

"Okay, well, maybe someone who isn't your parent can help." Mum stands and moves to my door. "I love you, Jess."

"Love you, too, Mum."

She leaves the door open slightly, and I take a deep breath. I don't want to see a psychologist, or talk about my dead sister. All I want is to curl up and sleep so everything will go away.

I rest my head against the bedhead and close my eyes. There's a knock on the front door upstairs. Mum's footsteps sound on the floorboards as she goes to answer it.

"Hi, Daniel. She's downstairs," Mums says.

I wait for Daniel to knock on my bedroom door before I open my eyes. He always knocks, even when the door is open.

"Come in," I say.

Daniel steps into my room, smiling, and it's contagious.

I can't help smiling back at him even though it's not something that comes easily for me anymore. He looks amazing in shorts and a surf T-shirt, and this time when my chest tightens it's not from pain, but from nerves.

Since Josephine's death Daniel has been really supportive, and I've grown to like him probably more than I should. Daniel and I have known each other for a long time, but he's two years older than me. There's no way he'd be interested in a girl the same age as his younger sister.

"I'm not going to ask how you are." Daniel sits on the bed with his legs crossed, mirroring me. "You look better though."

"I had a shower." I laugh.

"Showering is good. I didn't think it would be polite to tell you how stinky you were." He waves his hand in front of his nose as he screws it up, and I laugh harder.

Then I stop, because it's such a foreign sound, and it's not quite right coming from my mouth. Josephine's funeral is tomorrow. I should be preparing myself for the hard task of giving her eulogy.

"No, don't do that," Daniel says.

I stare at him, studying the lines that form between his eyebrows when he frowns.

"Don't do what?" I ask.

"Stop laughing." He leans on his legs with his elbows. "It's okay to be happy."

I shake my head and look at my hands. "No. It isn't. And I'm not."

"I am."

My breath hitches, and I look up at him in surprise. Happy is not a word I feel comfortable using. All happiness

left with Josephine.

"I don't think I know how to be happy anymore," I whisper.

"You need to stop being so hard on yourself."

"I deserve it." I look at my hands again.

Daniel sighs. "Jess, we've been over this. Josie's death was not your fault."

"You can't say that because you don't know what I did." I lean back against the bedhead and fold my arms over my chest, staring out the window so I don't have to see the questioning look in Daniel's eyes.

"Okay, so tell me. What did you do?"

The memory of Jarred's lips on mine, and how good it made me feel, sends a sharp pain through my heart. He was my sister's boyfriend, and he wasn't supposed to make *me* feel that way. But he did.

I've tried so hard not to think about what happened between us, and what I did to my sister. I haven't even spoken to Jarred since he dumped Josephine and stormed off. Maybe I should talk to him. Maybe he's hurting like I am.

I turn back to Daniel. "Telling you what I did won't change what happened."

He reaches out and takes my hands, rubbing the backs of them with his thumbs. "Talking about it might make you feel better." He pauses. "Nothing you did caused Josie's death."

"You're wrong." I pull my hands away and fold my arms again. "I'm a terrible person. I can't look at myself because all I see is her. And it reminds me of that night. All the time I'm reminded of what I did and how horrible and ugly—"

"You're not ugly, Jess," Daniel says. "You're the most beautiful girl I know."

I can't speak for a moment, because he's taken my breath away. "I was going to say my *heart* is horrible and ugly because of what I did."

Daniel takes a breath then lets it out between his teeth. "This is the last time I'm going to ask, and then I'll let it go." He studies me for a few heartbeats. "What did you do?

I lick my lips. Maybe I should tell him. Maybe it's best for him to find out and leave now, than for me to get too attached to him and have him walk out later.

"Jarred kissed me … and I didn't stop him. He thought I was Josie and I didn't tell him I wasn't until … after." I put my face in my hands. "I get it if you want to go now and never speak to me again."

Daniel doesn't respond, and it feels like forever before I peek through my fingers at him. He's frowning again, and I can't look away from the cute crease between his eyebrows.

"You're angry at me," I say.

He shakes his head. "Not at you, at … Do you like him?"

My mouth drops open. "No. I mean, I did once. But … no. He's Josie's boyfriend."

"Why did he think you were Josie?"

I close my eyes for a second then open them again. "We switched."

Daniel laughs, but it's not a humorous sound. "I remember you doing that when you were kids. It never ended well."

"Yeah," I say.

"And this is why Josie ran out that night? What you were fighting about?"

"It's also why I didn't want to tell you. Do you see now? It's my fault."

Daniel continues to study me, his face set in a deep frown, and tears prick at my eyes again like tiny hot needles. Will there ever be a day when I'll be able to stop crying? Right now that day seems so far away.

"You were not driving either of those cars," Daniel finally says. "You're not responsible for this, Jess. It just happened."

I don't argue, because even though I feel like Josephine's death is all on me, Daniel still refuses to accept it, and I'm tired of arguing with him.

"I won't be mad if you leave," I say.

"Okay, enough of that. I'm not leaving. Let's talk about something else." Daniel gets up from the bed and sits in the desk chair. "I have a question." He raises his eyebrows and I mimic him. "What's in the box? It wasn't here yesterday." He taps the top of the shoebox.

"Mum gave it to me this morning." I twist my fingers together and stare at it. "She's been collecting all the stuff people are leaving for Josie. Letters, notes, photos."

"From the telegraph pole on the corner?"

"Have you … been back?" I ask.

"Yeah. I've driven past a few times." Daniel's cheeks redden and he looks away. "I left some flowers for her a couple of days after …" He fidgets with the edge of his T-shirt.

"Why didn't you tell me?"

He shrugs and meets my gaze again. "I didn't want

to upset you. Have you been to see the pole? So many tributes. It's quite impressive."

I shake my head and look at my hands. "I don't think I'll be able to cope with that. Leaving Josie flowers though, that's really sweet of you."

The quiet hangs between us, and I glance at the box then back to my hands.

"This stuff with Jarred," Daniel says. "I'm not judging you. I don't know exactly what happened, but I know you. You can tell me anything. I would never stop talking to you, even if I was mad at you for something. We would always find a way to get past it. Just like you'll find a way to move forward. I want to help."

"Thanks, but I don't need your pity."

"It's not pity, Jess." Daniel leans back in the chair. "It's human decency. Besides, I've seen what walking away from someone does. It hurts. And I know how torn up Levi was when Mason died, and he couldn't go to Katie because he'd already walked away from her. I know what he did to my sister, and I don't ever want to do that to you."

My phone rings before I can respond. Veronica's name flashes on the screen. I really don't want to answer it, but she's been calling all week and I still haven't spoken to her. I let it ring out, again.

"You don't want to talk to her?" Daniel asks. "She was Josie's best friend, wasn't she?"

I sigh. "Yeah, she was."

Daniel picks up my phone from my side table and hands it to me. What will I say to Veronica though? Your best friend died because I kissed her boyfriend, he broke up with her, and we had a huge fight? Or I could just say hello.

I bring up her number and press call. It rings a couple of times before she answers.

"Jess?"

"Hey, Veronica."

"I've been worried about you," she says. "You haven't answered your phone."

"I know, I'm sorry." I take a deep, shuddering breath, because I feel the tears coming again. "I haven't felt up to it."

Veronica is quiet for a moment. "I've been really worried. Everyone's worried."

"I'm … trying to deal." I was about to say I'm okay, but I'm not.

"Well, if you want to get out and, you know, spend some time with us, I'm having a New Year's party, and it would be great if you and Stacey came. Dad's booked me two hotel suites on the harbour. We can hang out and take our mind off things." She sniffles and takes a breath. "Forget about the world for a while, you know? Forget about … all the shit we've been through."

Veronica is a tough girl, so when I hear her breathing hitch, it hurts my heart. "Okay, Ronnie. I'd love to come. I'll let Stacey know."

I don't want to go to any parties, I haven't even gotten through Christmas yet without Josephine, but I owe this to Veronica. She's hurting, too. Josephine wasn't just my sister; she had friends who love her as well.

"I'll see you tomorrow," Veronica says.

"Of course. I'll be there." I try to laugh, but the sound I make is more of a strangled sob.

Veronica ends the call, and I stare at the screen of my phone until it blinks off. Talking to Josephine's best friend has just made me sad all over again. How the hell am I supposed to pick myself up from this? What am I supposed to do?

Getting out of the house and going to a party might be a step forward, but what if Jarred is there? I'm pretty sure he will be. I have no idea how to act around him, or Josephine's other friends. What do I say to them? What do I say to Jarred?

I guess I'll find out tomorrow at Josephine's funeral.

I sigh, and push the New Year's party from my mind. I'll deal with it when I have to. But I'm glad Stacey can come with me.

Daniel touches my arm. "Hey, you back? You went somewhere for a moment there."

I meet his stare. "Yeah, I'm good. Just thinking. So much time for thinking lately."

"What did Veronica want to talk about?"

I set my phone on my side table. "She invited Stacey and me to a New Year's party. Her dad has booked her some hotel suites on the harbour."

"Sounds fun." Daniel smiles. "You'll have a great time."

"Maybe you can come. I can ring Ronnie back and ask her if you like?"

Daniel shakes his head. "I think spending time with Josie's friends will be good for you."

"What will you do?"

Daniel shrugs. "I've never been big on partying for New Year. Now that Mason's gone, I'd rather have a quiet one. He was always big on going out."

"Yeah, I remember."

Daniel holds my gaze for a heartbeat. "Maybe next New Year we can do something together."

"I'd like that."

Daniel smiles. "I have an idea. We can get out of the house for a bit. I'm taking Katie to the hospital this afternoon. Want to come?"

The hospital. Where Levi is.

I bite the inside of my cheek. "I'm not sure that's a good idea. I … Maybe seeing Levi right now isn't the best thing for me."

"Maybe." Daniel shrugs. "But it might help. He hasn't woken up yet, so you can yell at him as much as you want."

Daniel's trying to be funny and make me feel better, but it's not really working. "Another day?"

"I'll take you any time you want to go." Daniel stands. "You okay if I leave now?"

"Of course." I look up at him. "I'll see you tomorrow at … you know."

"Okay." He leans down and kisses me on the forehead.

His lips are soft and warm, and my stomach flutters. I wish he was kissing my lips instead, but he pulls back and walks to the door. Daniel turns and smiles, then disappears into the hallway. I rest my head against the bedhead and listen for the sound of the front door opening and closing. Minutes later Mum is standing in my doorway, a book in her hands and a small smile on her lips.

"Daniel has been coming by a lot," she says.

I haven't even had time to collect myself since his forehead kiss, and my stomach is still twitching with nerves.

"He's worried about me," I say.

"So am I." Mum comes and sits on the edge of the bed. "He's a lovely boy, Jess."

"He is pretty great." I smile, but then I check my expression because I can't be happy right now. I'm supposed to be mourning my sister. Her funeral is tomorrow.

"Don't frown. You don't need to feel bad for being happy about something." She reaches out and strokes my hair. "Josie would want you to be happy."

I nod, unable to talk because I'm on the verge of tears again, and any words I attempt will come out all jumbled.

"I brought you something." Mum keeps talking, as if she knows I can't right now. She hands me the book she's been holding. "It's a notebook. I thought you might like to write some things down. Get your thoughts out onto paper so they don't cloud your head. You could even write to Josie."

I take the notebook from her. The cover is a soft blue, like the sky on a clear summer's day. It's calming, and I rub my hand over it.

"Thanks." I open the notebook, and flip through the lined pages. The idea of filling them with words is both comforting and frightening.

I hug the notebook to my chest and smile at Mum. Maybe now I have a way to talk to my sister. Maybe now, I can tell her all the things I should have told her when she was alive.

Dear Josie

It's been a bit over a week since you died.

Mum and Dad want me to talk to someone about losing you. Mum made an appointment with a psychologist. I'm not sure it will help. She also gave me a notebook to write stuff in. She thinks maybe I'll be able to cope better by writing stuff down. I'm not entirely convinced about that either, because I don't think anything will help me recover from losing you. Even writing it on paper doesn't seem to make it real.

How do I survive this? How am I supposed to live in a world without you in it?

Anyway, I guess there's no harm in trying. Mum said I can write down anything I like, and I can write to you and talk to you. I think that's what I'm going to do. Write to you. Because how else do I tell you stuff?

I haven't really told Mum and Dad what happened that night. You know, the night we had our fight. I mean, I told them we argued, but I didn't tell them anything about Jarred and me, or how he broke up with you. The way Mum and Dad look at me sometimes makes me want to

scream until I lose my voice. Their eyes are always filled with so much pain. They don't blame me for the accident, but I wish they would.

I blame me.

Would they forgive me if they knew the truth?

What I did to you, and what happened as a result, is unforgiveable.

Losing you has broken me and left a gaping hole inside of me.

I'm not sure what else to write to you at the moment. I'm obviously not in the best mood. Thinking about you, and how I can't see you, is torture.

I probably should tell you about Daniel before I go. He was there when I found you. Just after your accident. He was driving me to come and find you to try to fix everything, but it was too late. He's been helping me deal with things. Talking to me, spending time with me. He's so sweet, and I really like him. But I can't be happy right now, because every time I smile or laugh, I remember that I'm smiling and laughing without you.

Then there's Levi. I should probably tell you about him as well. Looks like I do have some more stuff to say. He was part of your accident. He hit your car somehow, and Mum and Dad haven't really told me any details, but you know what happened after that. You probably know everything I'm telling you anyway.

I still don't want to believe this has happened. I guess it will really hit me tomorrow at your funeral. Maybe if I see you one last time I can accept what's happened. Or maybe I'll see you and completely lose it.

Everything is so screwed up, and I hope I can get

through tomorrow.

Hope.

It's a small word but it means so much.

Without you, what have I got left if I don't have hope? Hope that I can get through this. Hope that Mum and Dad will get through it, too. Hope that I'll be happy again one day. Hope that I can forgive myself for what I did.

But even if I do have hope for all these things, is it really enough?

Your loving sister, Jess xxx

You'll see

One thing I never thought I would have to do is say goodbye to my sister. We had so many plans to do so many things, and now that she's gone, I feel lost.

Today is the day of her funeral, and I'm lying in bed not knowing if I have the strength to even move my arms, let alone get out of bed and leave the house for the first time since she died. It's also HSC results day, but right now none of that stuff seems to matter. If I get through today, I can look at my results later.

I drag myself to the bathroom and have a shower, trying not to think about anything in particular. Especially not about the eulogy I'm going to give today. I haven't written anything down, because I can't sum up my sister's short life in a speech that will go for less than ten minutes. She deserves more time than that anyway. Jospehine

deserves forever.

There's still a sheet over the mirror in the bathroom I used to share with Josephine, so I quickly do my makeup as best I can with the tiny mirror in my compact. Looking at parts of my face doesn't set me off like it does when I see all of me. Still, by the time I'm finished my hands are shaking, and a heavy weight has settled into my stomach.

Back in my room, I dress in a cap-sleeved black top that has lace around the v-neckline, and a box-pleated black skirt that falls to my knees. It's warm today, so I slip my feet into a pair of black strappy sandals. I grab my phone and put it into my purse before stepping into the hallway.

Josephine's bedroom is next to mine, and instead of heading for the stairs on my right, I go left and walk along the hallway, stopping outside her closed door. I haven't been inside since before she died. I've heard Mum in there a couple of times, but until now I couldn't bring myself to go in.

I put my hand on the doorknob and twist, then slowly push the door open. Her room is just as it always is, only tidier. I glance from her bed to her desk, then to the mirror on her wardrobe door. It's the only one in the house that isn't covered.

From my vantage point in the doorway I can see half of my reflection. I quickly back out and close the door again, resting my forehead against the wood and closing my eyes.

"Please," I whisper, "help me get through today."

"Jess?" Mum says. "Are you ready?"

I straighten and look to where she's standing at the

bottom of the stairs. "Yeah."

She waits for me to get to her then wraps me in a tight hug. I close my eyes, not wanting to start crying now. I'm sure I'll do enough of that at the service. Mum must know I don't want to talk because she doesn't say anything. She just lets go and starts up the stairs.

I follow, and we find Dad in the kitchen, leaning against the bench with a coffee in one hand and a newspaper in the other. When he notices me, he quickly folds the paper and puts it down, but not before I catch a glimpse of Josephine's photo.

"Jess, sweetie. You look lovely," Dad says.

I walk to him and give him a hug.

Since Josephine died, I haven't asked Mum or Dad any questions about what happened. I haven't wanted to talk about it, and I figured they had enough to think about with going to the police station and the morgue, and organising the funeral. I didn't want to add to their distress.

But now, I realise I want to know what they know.

"Is there something in the paper about Josie? What have the police said about the accident?" I step away from Dad.

"We don't want you to worry about any of that," he says.

"But I want to know." I look from him to Mum and back again. "How did this happen?" I bite my bottom lip to stop from crying, and the coppery taste of blood fills my mouth. "Please," I whisper.

"There's not much to tell," Mum says. "Tests showed that Levi and Josie hadn't been drinking. But it seems ..."

I wait for Mum to keep talking. Her eyes fill with tears,

and one spills onto her cheek.

Dad takes a deep breath. "They said that after examining the scene, Josie may have run the stop sign."

I let the information sink in. Why would she have done that? Everyone who's a local knows that corner is blind. Running that sign would be like having a death wish, and I still can't get past the fact she shouldn't have even been there.

"It's my fault she was out driving. If I hadn't …" I take a shuddering breath, and wipe the tears from under my eyes. "She wasn't supposed to be there."

"Oh, sweetie." Mum wraps me up in her arms. "You have to stop doing this to yourself. Josie knew how to drive. This is not your fault."

Dad hugs us both, sandwiching me between him and Mum. We stand like that for a few heartbeats, and I feel safe inside our hug bubble. I don't know if I can go out and face everyone today. *How do I get through this?*

"Come on." Dad rubs my back. "Let's go and say goodbye to Josie."

We take the short drive to the local church. Dad avoids driving past the accident site, for which I'm grateful. I may never be ready to go back there. It's a little after nine, and the service doesn't start until ten o'clock, so the church carpark is quiet when we arrive. Dad takes a space close to the footpath leading to the main doors of the church.

When we pass inside, I stop at the end of the centre aisle for a moment and take it all in. The funeral director has everything ready to go, with bursts of yellow adorning the altar. Sunflowers, Josephine's favourite. Their brightness

makes me smile. I take a few steps and lean on the back of the last pew in the church. Mum and Dad start up the aisle towards the sanctuary.

Mum looks back. "Jess?"

"I'll come in a minute." I force a half-smile.

Mum nods and follows Dad the rest of the way to Josephine's casket, where it sits open, off to the right side of the altar. There's a small table at its foot. A vase filled with more sunflowers sits in one corner while a photo of Josephine is in the centre. It's our year twelve school photo, and the memory of that morning flashes into my mind. Josephine and I always made sure we wore our hair the same for school photos. She had straightened mine for me, and I smile as I hear her laughter in my head at whatever it was we were talking about. My smile falters, because I can't remember exactly what it was.

I slip into the back pew and fold my hands in my lap, watching Mum as she approaches the casket, peering over the side at my sister. Mum and Dad wanted an open casket, but I'm not sure *I* want to see her. What will she look like? Will she look normal, like herself? Or will she be all plastic and fake? I tell myself it's not really her; it's only the part that's been left behind. Still, do I have the courage to look at her face and say goodbye?

Mum steps back and Dad stands beside her, putting an arm around her shoulders. She leans into him, shaking, and it's seeing them like this that makes me get to my feet and walk down the aisle of the church. I should be with them. They shouldn't have to do this alone, and neither should I.

When I reach them, I sidle up to Dad and he puts his

other arm around my shoulders. I'm still not sure I want to look at Josephine. I'm standing so all I can see is the open lid of the casket, lined with white silky fabric.

"She's so peaceful." Mum steps forward again and peers in, her hand resting on the edge of the polished timber box.

Dad's breathing resonates through me, deep, shuddering breaths. He kisses the top of my head then lets go of me, moving to sit on the front pew. Mum raises her head and looks back at him, then goes and sits beside him.

The church is too quiet. My heart pounds in my ears. A part of me wants to run and not go through with looking into the casket, but another part of me thinks I might regret not saying goodbye to my sister face to face.

The last time I saw her she was dead in her car, covered in blood. I need an image to replace that, and although she'll still be dead, maybe seeing her here will help.

I wrap my arms around myself, and step up to the side of the casket. With a deep breath, I glance down, and Mum is right. Josephine looks peaceful. But she doesn't look like herself. Her skin is the wrong colour, and it's too smooth. I blink a few times, unable to believe how we got here. I choke back a sob and step away, putting a hand to my mouth.

The murmur of voices reaches my ears, and I turn to see people coming into the church. It won't be long until I have to get up and talk about my sister in front of everyone. I look back at Josephine lying in the box, her hands crossed on her chest as if they are protecting her heart.

"I miss you," I whisper, a tear rolling down my cheek. "I'm sorry."

"Jess, sweetie." Dad puts a hand on my shoulder. "Come and sit with us."

I let him lead me to the front pew. The three of us sit as people come up the aisle and pay their respects to Josephine. So many of them come and hug us, offering their condolences, and I try to smile and say thank you to all of them.

Veronica sits beside me and squeezes my hand. She doesn't say anything, and that small gesture means more to me than any words she could have said. Stacey comes and hugs me, too, but I don't see Karen, Katie, or Daniel. I get it though, not everyone wants to look at a dead body.

Jarred stops at the casket and stands with his hands in his pockets. He looks nice in his formal clothes. A navy blazer, pants, white shirt, and navy tie. When he turns, our eyes meet, and my fingers tingle with nerves. A deep frown mars his face. He nods in my direction, but he doesn't come over.

Slowly, the number of people paying their respects to Josephine dies down, and the priest comes to talk to us. The voices around me, including his, become a continuous drone.

"I'll call on you when it's time," the priest says. "Jessica?"

I meet his gaze. "Um ... Yeah, okay."

He nods and goes to Josephine, gently closing the casket lid before moving to stand at the top centre of the aisle. I glance over my shoulder at the people in the church. Every row is full. Daniel is sitting with Katie, Karen, and Stacey. They all offer me sympathetic smiles, but it's Daniel's eyes I lock my stare onto. I wish he was sitting beside me, holding my hand, holding me up.

You've got this, he mouths, and I nod then face the front again.

I want to be present during the service, but every time someone talks or reads aloud, my mind wanders to memories of my sister. I sit and stare at the box she's lying in, willing her to spring up and shout, 'Surprise, I tricked you'.

Before I know it, the priest is calling me. Dad pats my hand, and I get to my feet. The short walk to the pulpit seems like it takes forever, as if I'm moving in slow motion. When I stand and face the people in the church, so many faces stare back at me. So many have come to say goodbye to Josephine.

I lick my lips, tasting the salt from my tears as they run down my cheeks. I find Daniel's face and lock my gaze onto him, pretending I'm talking to only him, and there's no one else in the room.

"Josie was … She was my best friend." I take a shuddering breath. "Everyone would say we were like chalk and cheese. So different from each other." I grip the edge of the pulpit to steady myself, blinking to clear my blurry eyes. "But really, we weren't that different at all. We loved the same music, and the same clothes. Josie was just more outgoing than me. More … vibrant." Fresh tears spill onto my cheeks, and I swipe at them with my fingers. "If I was a cloud, she was the rainbow. So bubbly all the time. I miss her. I miss her smile and her laugh. She had such an infectious laugh." I turn and stare at the photo of my sister, sitting on the little table at the foot of her casket. I turn back to the congregation. "She was the other side of me. The better side."

I stare down at the flat timber of the pulpit in front of me. Little puddles of my tears have formed on the polished surface. I'm done. I can't say anymore, so without looking up at anyone, I make my way back to my seat. Dad moves so I can sit between him and Mum. He puts an arm around my shoulders and pulls me close.

The rest of the service goes by in a blur. I sit with my parents, gripping Mum's hand and leaning into Dad's side. Then it's time for him to get up. He joins three of my uncles at the foot of the altar, and they lift Josephine onto their shoulders. Mum and I stand to follow them down the aisle and out into the sunshine.

It's not fair that the day is so beautiful and Josephine isn't here to see it.

The pallbearers slide the casket into the back of the hearse, and we watch as it leaves for the cemetery.

"Let's spend a few minutes with everyone before we follow," Dad says.

Mum nods. We move from one person to the next. I let them hug and kiss me, nodding my thanks when needed but otherwise staying quiet. Someone touches my elbow, and I turn to face Katie. I've already cried so many tears, but more come as she folds her arms arounds me in a tight hug.

"I'm so sorry," she says.

I let her words hang for a moment, then ask, "Are you coming this afternoon?" I pull back and search her face. I'm not sure what I'm expecting. She wasn't exactly friends with my sister.

Katie presses her lips together. "I'd like to go and see Levi. They've taken him out of the coma. He might be

awake." She chews her bottom lip. "I can come if you'd like though?"

I shake my head. "No, it's okay. He needs you."

"But, you need me, too."

"I have Stacey." I look at my best friend. "And Karen. Levi needs you more than I do."

Katie gives me another hug. "I'll call you later."

I'm sad she doesn't want to come to the wake, but I understand. Levi is important to her, and he needs her right now. I can't imagine how Katie feels about him being the driver who hit Josephine's car. She's probably going through hell right now as well, and I haven't realised because I've been too busy dealing with my own anguish.

Daniel comes over and wraps me up in his arms. "I'll see you later, okay? I'll take Katie to the hospital then I'll be at yours."

I nod when he releases me. "There's plenty of time. We're going to the cemetery first."

"See you soon." Daniel kisses my forehead, then runs to catch up with Katie and his parents.

The touch of his lips on my skin lingers, and I smile as I watch him get into the car. On such a sad day he's managed to make me feel special and loved. He's the only person who has been able to make me feel a little better.

Mum and Dad come and find me to leave for the cemetery, and I tell Stacey and Karen I'll see them later. Dad drives, and by the time we get there Josephine's casket is ready and waiting beside her grave. A wreath of sunflowers adorns the centre of the lid. Her headstone is simple. Grey marble with gold lettering. *Josephine Bridget Hart. Loving daughter and sister. Forever in our hearts.*

The three of us wait for Josephine to be lowered into the ground. Then we each throw in a handful of dirt. The clumps hit the top of the casket with a thud. Dad hugs Mum, and holds my hand, as the caretaker begins to fill in the grave.

"We should get going," Dad says. "We have a party to throw for Josie."

I wrap my arms around myself as we walk to the car, glancing back at Josephine only once. "I love you," I whisper. I can't bring myself to say goodbye.

We're home for less than half an hour before the first people arrive. Then it's a steady stream of relatives and friends.

Everyone means well, but I find that I have to focus too hard on not bursting into tears, and it's exhausting. I'm numb to the words, 'I'm sorry'. Veronica, Jarred, and Geoff make a brief appearance. Jarred doesn't speak to me, and I think the others don't know what to say. They eat some food, talk to Mum and Dad for a few minutes, then leave.

Thankfully, I have Stacey and Karen. We sit in the lounge room watching everyone. Karen makes jokes about what my relatives are wearing and eating.

"Who wears red shoes to a wake?" she whispers.

"My aunt, obviously," I reply.

I try to laugh and go along with her. She's doing her best to keep my mind off things. I find I'm looking for Daniel anyway. He should be back from the hospital by now.

A few people leave, Karen and her parents among them. Karen hugs me fiercely goodbye.

"I'll see you soon," she says.

"Of course." I give her another hug.

After she's gone I turn to Stacey. "Think I need some air."

Stacey and I go outside to the deck that overlooks the bush valley at the back of our house. We sit on the chair swing together, moving slowly back and forth.

"I know everyone has been asking how you are today," Stacey says. "But really, Jess. Are you … okay?"

I shrug and stare at the trees. "No, yes. No. I don't know. I mean, Josie could be a bitch sometimes, but dying? She wasn't supposed to do that." And then the words just pour out. "You know I love you, Stace, and you're my best friend, but she was my sister. We were best friends by default. We loved each other unconditionally. And I especially loved the Josie I knew. The one who cut all the bullshit when it was just the two of us. I mean, we had our fair share of fights …" I trail off, because a fight with my sister is what led us here.

Stacey puts an arm around my shoulders. "I know."

We sit and swing. I listen to the voices inside, all joining together into one drone.

"Veronica asked us to a New Year's party," I say after a couple of minutes. "Want to go?"

"Another one of Veronica's parties." Stacey gets to her feet and stretches, moving to lean on the deck railing. "Sounds like a blast."

Daniel appears, and I jump up from the chair swing. Stacey looks from me to him and back again.

She comes and hugs me. "I'll see you tomorrow, okay?"

"Thank you," I whisper, hugging her back.

Daniel waits for Stacey to leave before he speaks. "You look tired." He shoves his hands in his pockets.

"I am." I force a smile. "You missed most of the fun."

"How many people asked you how you're doing?"

I actually laugh. "Pretty much everyone here."

"Want me to sit with you?" Daniel points to the chair swing.

"I'd rather go to my room where it's quiet."

Daniel closes the gap between us and slips his hand into mine. "Come on then."

He leads me to the top of the outside stairs, and I follow him down to the yard below. We walk through the backyard and go inside via the laundry door. In my room, I flop onto the bed and lie on my side, kicking my sandals off.

From my pillow I stare at the shoebox sitting on my desk. Mum has been adding more notes and photos to it, and the lid doesn't quite sit on properly anymore. Maybe I should start reading and looking at what's in there, but not today. I'm not sure I can handle any more tears. I close my eyes and snuggle down into my pillow.

"Want me to leave so you can rest?" Daniel asks.

I reach for his hand and he clasps my fingers. "Stay until I fall asleep?"

"Of course."

"I'm tired of crying." I keep my eyes closed. "I cry less when you're here."

"Glad I can help." His words linger for a moment before he speaks again. "Every day will be better than the last, Jess. You'll see."

Dear Josie

Today was your funeral. It was hard. But looks like I got through it, since I'm still here.

After the service, a lot of people came to the house for your wake. That's a weird word, isn't it? Especially since you will never 'wake' up again.

I had to look it up in the dictionary. 'Wake' means to become roused from sleep, but it also means to keep watch or vigil over. Doubly weird since by the time everyone was at our house you were already in the ground under a huge pile of dirt.

How can I watch over you when you're six feet under? Are you watching over me?

Anyway, so many people came and so many people paid their respects. Everyone was really nice, but it was exhausting.

I ended up sneaking off to my room with Daniel. And no, we didn't do anything. He just stayed with me until I fell asleep. Mum and Dad must have let me sleep through dinner, because now it's almost midnight and the house is quiet.

Too quiet.

And I'm sad that I can't go into your room and climb into bed with you like I used to when we were little.

I woke up, and for a second I didn't know where I was. I wanted to find you, but then I remembered you're not here anymore. When I saw the blanket hanging over my wardrobe door, it all came back to me.

Have I told you I've covered all the mirrors in the house? I can't look at myself without crying or having a panic attack. When I look at myself, all I see is you. It's like I'm being punished for what I did to you. I'm forever destined to be reminded that I killed my twin sister.

I feel ugly, but I think you're beautiful.

I wish you were here so I could talk to you instead of writing it down. I'll try to write again tomorrow.

Right now, I need more sleep.

Your exhausted sister, Jess xxx

Reminds me of her

ootsteps sound on the stairs, and a few moments later Mum is standing in my doorway.

"Jess, sweetie, you need to get up and get dressed. Your appointment is in a little over an hour."

I peek out from under my blanket. "Please don't make me go."

Mum sighs. "It will be good for you. I'll see you in the kitchen in ten minutes."

She disappears into the hallway, and I listen as she walks back upstairs, her footfalls sounding on the timber floorboards above.

My first appointment with the psychologist is today.

I don't want to go.

Leaving the house for Josephine's funeral was hard enough. Going out to talk to someone about my dead sister

seems like the most impossible thing to do right now.

I drag myself out of bed and have a quick shower. Back in my room, I run a comb through my wet hair and leave it out to dry. Then I dress in a plain white singlet top and denim skirt, slipping my phone into my back pocket. I don't bother with any makeup.

When I walk into the kitchen, there's a plate of honey toast and a bowl of yoghurt with fruit on the bench, even though it's well past breakfast. Mum is at the sink rinsing dishes and stacking them in the dishwasher.

"Take it into the dining room." Mum glances over her shoulder. "Dad's waiting for you."

"Thanks," I say, forcing a smile.

Since Josephine died, my appetite has been non-existent, but I pick up the plate and go into the next room, taking the seat to Dad's left.

He puts his paper down and takes a sip of his coffee, checking his watch. "It's nice to see you out of your room."

I pick up a piece of toast and take a bite so I don't have to reply. What am I supposed to say anyway? I like it in my room? I know it's almost lunch time? Leave me alone to mourn in my own way?

The toast feels thick in my throat, so I put the rest of the piece back on the plate. The spoon in the yoghurt clinks against the side of the bowl when I pick it up. I can only stomach one mouthful. It tastes too sour.

"Are you going to dry your hair?" Dad asks.

"No." I take another bite of toast.

"Come on, Jess. Please put some effort in."

Effort?

Getting out of bed in the first place was hard. Anger

hangs like a heavy stone in my stomach. Dad's words have struck a chord. I eat more of my toast, then drop it on the plate and stand. The chair legs scrape on the floorboards.

"I'm not hungry." I take my plates to the kitchen. "Are we going now?" I ask Mum.

She studies my face, then glances over my shoulder towards the dining room. "Everything okay?"

"Yep." I turn and head for the front door, yanking it open.

Mum and Dad follow me to the car. I don't make eye contact with them as I get in, slouching down into the back seat and staring out the window, waiting for this to all be over.

"Don't forget your manners today, Jess," Dad says.

"Whatever," I mumble.

He turns in his seat, one hand on the steering wheel and the other gripping the headrest on Mum's side. "You need to snap out of it, young lady. The funeral is over. We have to try to move on."

I glare at him. "Move on? Josie is dead, Dad. How the hell do we move on from that?"

"Let's just go, okay?" Mum says calmly, putting her hand on Dad's knee.

Dad clenches his jaw and faces the front again.

I want to go back to my room.

I don't want to talk to some stranger about my feelings.

I want to talk to Daniel.

Dad starts the car and reverses onto the road. I don't know the man sitting behind the wheel driving. He is never angry like this. But then I've never been one to act how I have been lately. Josephine's death has ruined all of us.

No one speaks for the first ten minutes of the trip. Then Dad starts talking to Mum as if I'm not even here.

"I want to be in the meeting," he says.

"I think we should let Jess go in by herself if she wants to," Mum replies.

"I want to know what they say to her."

"I'm not sure that's any of our business."

"Of course it's our business, she's our daughter."

"And she's old enough to decide what she wants to do."

"Most days she won't even leave her room," Dad says. "You've seen her. She's in no state to make decisions."

The stone in my stomach hardens. "Hello, I'm sitting right here, Dad."

He sighs and grips the steering wheel, looking at me in the rear-view mirror. "I want to help you, but you need to help yourself as well."

"We both want to help." Mum turns in her seat and looks at me.

I press my lips together, and go back to staring out the window, watching other cars pass by and trying to see the people inside them. Have any of them lost someone they love? Are they on their way to talk to a complete stranger about death? Are their families struggling like mine?

Dad parks the car, and I follow him and Mum into the psychology centre. It's a red-brick building with dark windows like gaping eyes. Dad stops in the foyer to read the sign, then we take the stairs to the second floor. I stare at my feet as we walk. I don't know who I'm seeing. I haven't even thought to ask for a name. We pass a few suites before Dad pushes a glass door open and holds it for Mum and me.

Mum steps up to the front desk. "Hello. Jessica Hart to see Doctor Lewinsky."

"Take a seat," the receptionist says, smiling. "Won't be long."

The three of us sit in hard plastic chairs and wait.

My anger stone turns to a nausea puddle, sloshing around in my stomach. I *really* don't want to do this.

A door to the left of the reception desk opens, and a man with a bald head and black-rimmed glasses steps through. "Mr and Mrs Hart. Jessica? Please …" He moves to the side, gesturing towards the room with his hand.

"Do you mind if we come?" Mum touches my arm.

I shrug. *Whatever.*

"I'd like to see all of you, then we can separate," the doctor says.

Mum and Dad stand. I hesitate, then take a deep breath and follow. We go into a dimly lit office, decked out with dark timber furniture, a plush lounge setting, and old-fashioned brocade curtains. A couch faces two armchairs with a coffee table in between. There's a polished wooden chair at one end with a large desk behind it.

"I'm Doctor Lewinsky, head psychologist." He shakes Mum and Dad's hand, then points to the two armchairs. "Please sit. Jessica, why don't you take a seat on the couch?"

Mum and Dad settle into the chairs. I glance at the bookshelf that lines the wall behind the desk. So many books. How could Doctor Lewinsky have possibly read them all? Dad clears his throat, and I turn my attention back to the couch.

It seems so big.

I tuck myself into the corner farthest away from Doctor

Lewinsky, feeling exposed, as if I'm under a microscope. I ball my hands into fists, resting them on my knees. My nails dig into my palms.

"Jessica." Doctor Lewinsky smiles. "It's nice to see you today. How are you feeling?"

Seriously? That's his first question?

I frown and look at my hands. "Fine."

"Can you tell me why you're here?"

He knows why I'm here.

"She needs help dealing with her sister's death," Dad says.

"I think it would be nice if Jessica spoke for herself," Doctor Lewinsky says. "There will be plenty of time for you, and Mrs Hart, to chat with me as well."

I glance up. Dad's brow is creased, and I can tell he wants to say more, but he doesn't.

"Jessica," Doctor Lewinsky continues. "What brings you here to see me today?"

I blow a breath out between my lips. If I don't answer, this will just take longer. "I … My sister died, and I … She died."

"And you're having some trouble coping?"

I nod, a lump forming in my throat.

"I'm here to help you in any way I can," Doctor Lewinsky says. "We have an excellent team of psychologists and counsellors. Before we go any further, there's someone I would like you to meet. Would it be okay with you if she sits in with us?" I nod again, and Doctor Lewinsky goes behind his desk. He presses a button on his phone. "Penny, would you like to join us now?"

"Of course." A soft female voice comes out of the phone

speaker.

A moment later the door opens, and a small woman with sleek black hair and delicate features enters.

"Hello," she says.

"This is Penny Ling, our grief counsellor," Doctor Lewinsky says. "She's an excellent listener."

Both of them smile.

Dad gets to his feet and holds out his hand. "Pleased to meet you, Doctor Ling."

She shakes his hand and then Mum's. "Please, call me Penny."

Penny sits at the other end of the couch. "It can be difficult to cope with what you've been through. We're here to help." She smiles again.

"In order to understand you and your situation a bit better, Jessica, we'd like to ask you some questions," Doctor Lewinsky says. "Would that be okay?"

I chew the inside of my cheek and nod, yet again.

"Perfect." He picks up a notepad and pen, then sits in the wooden chair. He crosses his legs and rests the notepad on his knee. "Can you tell us, have you talked about your emotions with anyone since your sister died? Is there someone you feel comfortable confiding in?"

I glance at Mum and Dad. I haven't really told them anything about anything. Only that I fought with Josephine, and I think her dying is my fault. I open my mouth to tell the doctor about Daniel, but snap it shut again.

I shake my head. "No. I haven't talked to anyone."

"But she writes in a notebook," Mum says. "And she has Dan—"

"Mum." I glare at her.

I'm not ready to share this stuff with two complete strangers.

"A journal is a wonderful way to help you deal with your situation, Jessica." Doctor Lewinsky smiles. "How have you been sleeping?"

I shrug. "Fine." *Not very well.*

He scribbles something on the pad. "Are you eating well?"

I have no appetite. "Yeah, I guess."

"She doesn't eat much," Dad says. "And she's rarely out of bed before lunch time."

Why are my parents insisting on speaking for me?

Doctor Lewinsky pauses, and I wait for him to reprimand Dad again. Instead he asks, "Is that true, Jessica?"

"I like it in my room," I say. "And I eat when I'm hungry."

More note taking.

What's he writing?

"That's good." He looks up at me. "Your room is understandably a place where you feel safe. It might be helpful though to go outside and get some fresh air every now and then. Even if you just sit and listen to the sounds around you. Do you have a place at home where you can do that?"

"We have a chair swing," I say.

"Perfect." Doctor Lewinsky makes more notes. "Your parents have told me you're having trouble looking in the mirror. Can you tell us why?"

I blink a few times to stop the tears that are burning my eyes. "Because I look like her," I whisper.

Doctor Lewinsky writes something else on the notepad.

The room is quiet. I concentrate on my breathing,

because I need something to focus on other than talking about my dead sister. Pain pricks my palms as I clench my fists tighter.

"We all deal with grief in different ways," Penny says. "Josephine was your identical twin, so it's understandable that you feel a range of emotions when you look at yourself."

Range of emotions? *Mostly guilt and hatred.*

"Moving forward, I'd like you to spend some time each week talking to Penny." Doctor Lewinsky stands and puts the notepad on the desk behind him. "I'm going to have a chat with your parents now, so we'll leave you to get started. You can stay in my office for today since you already look quite comfortable." He smiles at me, then glances from Mum to Dad and back again before moving towards the door.

My parents take the hint and stand to follow. Doctor Lewinsky opens the door for them, and they all leave the room. I'm alone with Penny now, and although she seems nice, she's still a stranger who I'm expected to bare my soul to.

Penny moves to one of the armchairs. "How are you feeling about being here, Jessica?"

When I make eye contact with her, she smiles, and it makes me feel a little more at ease. She has a friendly face. And there's only one person studying me now, rather than four. I try to relax back into the lounge.

"I feel … lost," I say.

"Again, that's very understandable." She pauses. "Can you tell me what you hope to gain from your sessions with me?"

I frown. "I'm not sure. I don't really want to be here."

"That's okay. Often it can take some time to adjust to talking to someone you don't know." Penny crosses her legs and stares at me. "How about you tell me something about Josephine. What did she like?"

"Sunflowers," I say. "She loved sunflowers."

Penny nods, and I relax a little more.

She continues to ask me questions for the next half an hour, and I find myself trusting her more with every answer I give.

"Have you visited the accident site yet?" Penny asks.

"No." I shake my head. "No ... I can't."

"How do you think it would make you feel if you did?"

My breath gets stuck in my chest. The image of Josephine in her car fills my head, and I can't get it out. I squeeze my eyes closed and pinch the bridge of my nose.

"It hurts too much," I manage to say. "I can't even look in the box. How can I go back there?"

"Box?" Penny asks. "Can you tell me about that?"

Crap.

I don't want to talk about this.

"Do I have to?"

"You don't have to do anything you don't want to."

We look at each other for a long moment. Penny's eyes are warm and patient. She's trying to help me, and I keep resisting when it gets hard.

"Mum gave me a shoebox," I finally say. "It has letters, and notes, and pictures. For Josephine. People have been leaving them at the telegraph pole."

Penny holds my gaze. "I would like you to consider visiting the site of the accident. And maybe reading some of the tributes people have left for your sister. You don't have to do it today, or tomorrow, or even next week. In your own time. But it may help your healing process. Help you push through the darkness.”

“Maybe.” I break our stare and look over to the bookshelves, pretending to study them so I don’t have to make eye contact with Penny.

“Our time is almost up,” Penny says after a minute. “But I would like to ask you one more question before you go. Your mum was about to say someone’s name before. Do you think you can share it with me? Is it someone special to you?”

I tuck my hair behind my ear and chew on my thumbnail. “His name is Daniel,” I say. “He was there when I found …”

“How does Daniel make you feel?”

Amazing. “He sits with me and … I just like spending time with him. When he’s there, everything feels less … bad.”

“That’s wonderful,” Penny says. “Having a normal teenage relationship after a tragic event is healthy.” Penny stands. “It was nice to spend time with you, Jessica. I’m looking forward to seeing you again next week.”

I get to my feet, and exhaustion washes over me. Talking about Josephine for so long has left me drained. I blink back tears as Penny shows me to the door. Mum and Dad are waiting at reception, and I follow them out of the building to the car. It’s not until we’re halfway home that the questions start.

“How do you feel?” Mum asks.

“Fine,” I say.

“What did you talk about?” Dad looks at me in the rear-view mirror.

I glare at him. *None of your business.*

"Stuff."

My phone vibrates, and I pull it from my back pocket. When I see Daniel's name on the screen, I smile. He always lifts my spirits.

Daniel: Can I come over?

Me: Of course. Give me 15?

Daniel: CU soon

"Who is that?" Dad asks.

"Daniel," I reply. "He's coming over this afternoon."

"Ask him to stay for dinner," Mum says. "We can have an early barbeque."

Dad swings the car into the driveway. "Might keep you out of your room," he mumbles.

My short-lived good mood drops again. Maybe Dad is having a bad day, and he's not coping so well either. He certainly hasn't been himself.

"I'll ask him," I say.

We go inside, and instead of heading straight to my room like I want to, I stay upstairs. I feel out of place though, and I wander from the kitchen to the lounge room, then out to the back deck.

Spend time outside, Doctor Lewinsky said.

I sit in the chair swing and move it slowly back and forth. It's the middle of summer, and the air is heavy with heat. A breeze stirs the leaves in the trees, and a kookaburra laughs. How long has it been since I've stopped to listen to the world around me?

"Hey, you," Daniel says, stepping onto the deck. "Can I sit?"

I smile. "Of course."

He eases into the swing beside me.

"How was your day?" I ask.

"Nothing special. Hospital with Katie. A shift at work. Just the usual. How about you?"

"The same."

I'm not ready to tell him I'm seeing a counsellor. I should, but my first session was emotionally draining, and I don't want to talk about it right now. If I talk about it, then it's real. That's probably why talking about Josephine is so hard. It makes her death realer than it already is.

"I was surprised to find you up here," Daniel says. "You're usually in your room. Are you feeling better?"

The swing rocks slowly back and forth, and I stare at my hands. "Not really. But I'm trying." I take a shuddering breath. "Mum wants to know if you'd like to stay for dinner."

"I'd love that." Daniel reaches over and takes my hand, giving it a gentle squeeze. He grins, then pushes his feet into the deck. We go back fast and fly forwards. I grip the edge of the seat and laugh.

"Again?" Daniel asks.

"Gently this time," I say, still laughing.

"Okay." He grins.

I tuck my feet up onto the chair, and let Daniel rock us back and forth. For a little while we just sit, staring at the bush below, listening to the noises around us. It's calming, but when we go back inside, everything comes crashing down.

The house is full of Josephine.

Everywhere I go, and everything I do, reminds me of her.

Dear Josie

The other day I had my first appointment with the psychologist. When we arrived, I was in a bad mood. Maybe that's why I didn't like it so much. Dad had said something mean before we left. But I don't need to tell you what it was. I didn't really talk to the psychologist guy much. It was weird, having some stranger ask me questions. Questions I didn't want to answer. Questions I didn't know how to answer.

He thinks Mum giving me this notebook to write stuff in was a good idea, so here I am, writing stuff down, and telling you things.

Anyway, I have a solid booking now with a grief counsellor. A different person to this psychologist guy I saw, but at the same centre. Her name is Penny, and she sat in with us while the psychologist did the initial assessment on me. Or at least that's what I think he did. He took notes. I'm not sure if I passed or failed. I guess I failed if I have to see someone every week.

At the moment I don't need medication, which is good because I don't want drugs. I still want to feel like me, if

I can figure out what that's actually supposed to feel like.

The psychologist told Mum and Dad no meds because I'm sleeping okay. Which I'm actually not, but I told them I am.

All I want to do is sleep.

When I'm asleep it doesn't hurt.

All the pain is there when I'm awake.

The good thing about being awake though …

Daniel.

I really like him, Josie. Is that bad? Is it bad that I'm having all these awesome feelings over a guy when you're not here for me to share them with? Is it okay for me to feel happy about Daniel, when I feel so sad most of the time?

I don't know.

I did tell the grief counsellor about Daniel. She seems to think my relationship with him is healthy. It's funny how they talk all serious. Not my relationship with him is great, or awesome. It's healthy.

What does that even mean?

Does she want me to use him to get better? Because I'm not sure I like the idea of using Daniel for anything. I want to like him because I genuinely like him, not because it's healthy for me to.

Oh, and I told the counsellor about the box of stuff from the accident site. She thinks I should go back there for a visit, and she wants me to read the stuff in the box. Apparently it will help me push through my grief and come out the other side feeling better. I mean, really? How will reliving my biggest, darkest nightmare make me feel better?

Your confused sister, Jess xxx

I'm not sure you can

Since Daniel stayed for dinner, the days have blended together, and I don't feel much better, even after seeing Penny. My last session made me angry, because talking about Josephine is supposed to be helping. It's not. It doesn't. Talking about her just makes me mad at myself for what happened, and frustrated that I'm not feeling any better.

The only time I feel anything close to happy is when I'm with Daniel.

I keep asking myself how long it's supposed to take to get over losing a loved one. People say every day is supposed to get a little bit easier, but it doesn't seem to.

I'm still just as broken as the day she left.

And I hate myself for it.

Daniel gives me updates on Levi only when I ask. He

says he thinks he's doing well. They've taken him off the respirator, so that must be a relief for Katie.

Still, I often ask myself, why did he live and Josephine didn't? Am I selfish to sometimes wish it was him who died? If I had the choice, would I trade his life for hers? And if I say yes, what sort of person does that make me?

My university letters came a few days ago. I got into my first choice, but I have no idea if I even want to go to uni anymore. I was going to defer for a year anyway. Josephine and I wanted to travel. Now she's gone, nothing else seems important.

I'm sitting here on my bed thinking about all of this, tying my stomach into knots, waiting for Daniel to come back. He was here this morning, but he had to pick Katie up from the hospital. I'm not sure he wanted to leave me, since I haven't been doing so well. I do better when he's here. Without him, everything seems so much harder.

A knock sounds on the front door upstairs. I rest my head against the bedhead and listen.

"Jess is in her room," Mum says.

"How is she?" It's Katie's voice.

"She's … not coping very well," Mum says. "She won't look in the mirror, and I can't get her out of her room. Maybe …" Mum goes quiet.

"We'll just sit with her for a bit," Daniel says.

He's back, and I smile. He already knows I'm a broken mess.

I move from the bed to my desk chair and stare out the window, waiting for Katie and Daniel to come downstairs. I'm vaguely aware I'm still in my pyjamas, and my room is a shambles. When they come in, I catch Katie's expression

from the corner of my eye. She's looking at the towel taped over the mirror on my wardrobe door. I needed the throw rug, so I used duct tape to put a bath towel up. It hasn't fallen off yet.

Katie sits on the bed in front of me. "Hey. We thought you might like some company."

"Maybe we could go for a walk?" Daniel sits beside her.

I focus on the two of them for a moment. "I don't feel up to a walk."

Katie stares out the window. "We could go upstairs and sit on the balcony. Look at the trees and listen to the birds."

I force a smile. "Can we just sit here?"

"Sure," Katie says.

Daniel moves on the bed until he's sitting with his back against the wall under the window. Katie seems a little lost. She twists her fingers together, then stands and busies herself tidying my room. She sets things right on my bedside table, putting a few dirty tissues in the bin, then she bundles up the dirty clothes on the floor and puts them in the hamper, taking the basket out to the laundry.

While she's gone, I move to the bed and sit beside Daniel. When I'm close to him, I feel better, and I lean into him. He puts his arm around my shoulders, and my stomach flutters. How I felt when I kissed Jarred doesn't even come close to how I feel about Daniel.

"Feeling okay?" he asks.

"Better now." I smile up at him.

Daniel shifts a little and stares into my eyes. He licks his lips, and my stomach doesn't flutter this time, it rolls.

Big waves of nerves crash through me. I turn my body towards him, and he leans closer. I hold my breath.

"Close your eyes," Daniel whispers.

I blink a few times then do as he says.

When his lips press against mine they are soft and tentative, his touch sending little shockwaves across my skin.

He pulls away, ending our kiss too soon. I stare into his eyes again, searching them for any sign that I've done something to make him pull back.

"Was that … okay?" Daniel asks.

I let out a breath and nod. "Yes." *Oh God, yes.*

He smiles and kisses me again, this time with more urgency. I part my lips and move with his, taking his lead, hoping I'm doing this right. Daniel grips my hip and pulls me closer. I tangle my fingers into his hair.

"Katie?" Karen's voice whispers in the hallway. "What are you doing?"

"Oh my God, you scared me," she whispers back.

This time, I break our kiss. I pull back from Daniel and stifle a giggle. He grins and kisses my forehead.

"Thought I should be quiet." Karen's voice is low. "Since you're already spying on Jess."

"Why are we whispering?" Stacey is here, too. "What's going on?"

"Daniel and Jess … He kissed her," Katie whispers again, her voice getting slightly louder.

"What?" Karen blurts.

"Maybe we should leave," Katie says.

"You don't have to go," Daniel calls, still grinning. "You think we can't hear you?"

Katie steps into the doorway. "I know you heard Karen."

Karen laughs and pushes her best friend into my bedroom. Stacey follows them.

"Hi girls," Daniel says.

Katie sits in my desk chair, throwing her brother a sideways glance. Karen and Stacey drop a shopping bag each onto the floor.

"I'm glad we're all here," Karen says. "Stacey and I brought supplies."

"We've got chocolate, and lollies, and chips, and tea, and DVDs." Stacey kneels, taking out the contents from one of the bags.

"All the stuff we need for an afternoon in." Karen sits beside Stacey.

"I should probably go," Daniel says. "You girls look like you have a busy afternoon ahead of you."

I chew my bottom lip, and stare at him. I don't want him to go, but if he doesn't feel comfortable staying with all of us, then I'm not going to stop him. I slip my hand into his and hold it tightly, hoping he can feel how much I want him to stay.

"Don't be stupid," Karen says, glancing from me to Katie. "You can stay."

They're all probably wondering what the hell is going on between Daniel and me, since I haven't told any of them how I feel about him. I think it's pretty obvious I like him though, since Katie caught us kissing.

Karen opens a big block of chocolate and passes it to Katie. She takes a few pieces then throws it onto the bed. I let go of Daniel's hand so I can break some off for the both of us. We continue to stuff our faces with junk food,

and talk about Christmas.

"Anyone going away?" Karen asks.

"Nope, we'll be at home," Katie says. She smiles at Daniel.

I shake my head. "Staying home, too. Mum cancelled everything."

I'm secretly glad she did. Trying to cope with visiting relatives is the last thing I want to do right now, especially since I don't have Josephine to keep me company. The thought of doing anything without my sister seems unbearable.

"We have to go up the coast to Nan's place." Stacey crinkles her nose. "It's always noisy."

"Well, I'm being dragged down south to my aunt's," Karen says. "Four nights of sleeping on the floor in my cousin's room."

"You love it." Katie grins.

"Yeah, the little rug rats are kinda cute."

"What's everyone getting for Christmas?" Stacey asks.

"I want my own car." Karen puts a piece of chocolate in her mouth. "But that's never going to happen. I usually ask for money so I can go shopping at the sales."

"Socks," Daniel says, smiling. "I need socks."

Everyone laughs, even me, and it feels nice to be having a normal conversation with my friends.

"The presents don't matter so much," Katie says. "I just like being with fam …"

She stops before she finishes the word, but we all know exactly what she was about to say. The air fills with an uncomfortable quiet. My smile falls away, and I snuggle against Daniel, looking at my hands as if they

are the most interesting thing in the world right now. I take a deep breath in an effort to hold back the tears. I've managed not to cry much today, and I don't want to start now.

"I'm sorry ... Jess, I ... I'm sorry." Katie's voice is filled with sadness.

"It's okay." I keep my eyes trained downward, and tuck my hair behind my ear. "Family is really important. And friends are, too." When I look up at Katie, her expression is pained, and I have to remember she's doing her best in this sucky situation, too. "How's Levi?"

Katie opens her mouth, but then closes it again. Finally, she says, "He's ... they say he'll be fine." She looks away from me and hugs her knees, pulling her feet up onto the desk chair. "He's not awake properly yet, so I haven't ... he hasn't talked to anyone."

No one speaks. Outside, a kookaburra laughs, and I want to tell it there's nothing funny about any of this. I look at my hands again, and concentrate on Daniel's warmth beside me.

"Oh!" Karen breaks the silence. "I got two acceptance letters yesterday."

"That's great," Daniel says. "Where to?"

"One for Newcastle, and one for Macquarie."

"I got a letter from Sydney Uni," Stacey says, and I look up.

"Let me guess." Katie rests her chin on her knees. "Vet science?"

"Yep." Stacey is grinning so much her cheeks must hurt.

"What course were you accepted into, Karen?" Katie asks.

"Psychology." She opens a fresh packet of chips, stuffing a handful in her mouth before passing the bag to Stacey. "Think I'll go to Newcastle."

Psychology. I had never given it much thought as a profession until I had to see a psychologist myself, and I haven't told anyone I'm seeing a grief counsellor. Not even Daniel.

"I got into Newcastle as well," I say. "For their communications degree. I think I'd like a career in journalism … someday."

"What do you mean, someday?" Katie asks.

"I've always wanted a year off to travel. Josie was going to come with me. Now, I don't know what I want to do. With Josie gone …" I shrug, and stare at a spot on the bed. "What's the point? Why go to uni, or travel, or do anything, when I could die tomorrow? Any of us could …"

From the looks on my friends' faces I've hit a nerve, and the room fills with sadness. I'm not sure if it's theirs, or all of mine spilling out so there's enough for all of us.

"Have you opened your letters yet?" Karen pipes up again, raising her eyebrows at Katie.

"No, she hasn't." Daniel shifts beside me, a frown marring his forehead, and takes the chips from Stacey, putting some in his mouth.

Katie stares at Daniel, her expression as sad as I feel.

"Maybe Jess has the right idea," she says. "What *is* the point?"

Our conversation is a little stilted for a while. No one seems to be in a particularly good mood. There's a lot of looking around the room but not at each other. I close my eyes and rest my head on Daniel's shoulder, and

even though I see images of Josephine in my mind, right now dealing with that seems easier than talking to my friends about anything. Especially about how I'm not coping so well.

"I should get home," Karen says. "You look like you could use some rest, Jess."

When I open my eyes, I catch her glancing sideways at Katie.

"Yeah. You must be exhausted." Katie gets to her feet. "We'll see you soon?"

I nod, and they tidy up the empty food packets before heading into the hallway, leaving Stacey with Daniel and me.

Stacey snaps off a few squares of chocolate from the last block. "Ugh. I think I've eaten too much crap." But she still puts it into her mouth. "I'm going to head off, too." She gets up and looks at Daniel. "Look after my girl, yeah?"

"Of course," he says.

I smile at my best friend, and hope she knows how thankful I am. I love her, and I want to spend time with her, but after kissing Daniel, I think we have a few things to talk about. Like how we really feel about each other, and if he can handle being with someone as broken as I am. I want him to know I'm not falling for him just because he's here. I've been falling for him ever since I knew what boys were. But he's older, and I never in a million years would have thought he'd be interested.

Stacey gives me a quick hug before she leaves, then Daniel and I sit quietly for a while. I rest my head against his chest and listen to the sounds of his breathing and heartbeat, counting each breath and each thump.

"Daniel," I finally say, unable to look at him because my cheeks are so hot. "What did that kiss mean? Are we … Do you … How …?"

Daniel lifts my chin with his finger, and when I look at him, he's smiling.

"I really like you, Jess. I have for a long time." He leans in and kisses me softly then pulls back. "I thought maybe you guessed that."

"I like you, too. But I don't want you to think it's just because you're here. I … you …" I tuck my hair behind my ear and chew the inside of my cheek.

Daniel plays with the ends of my hair, rolling the strands between his fingers. "Can we go with it and see what happens?"

I nod and rest my head back on his shoulder. "Okay."

A few minutes later, Daniel asks, "Have you looked in the box yet?"

I raise my head and sit forward, staring at the shoebox on my desk. The lid is cocked due to the box being over full.

"I'm still not ready," I say.

Daniel rubs my back. "Okay. Why don't we go for a walk? Get some fresh air."

I pull my knees up and rest my cheek on them. "I don't know. I like it in here."

Daniel reaches out and tucks my hair behind my ear. "What about the Christmas tree? Have you put it up yet?"

I shake my head. "None of us have been in a very Christmassy kind of mood."

"Well." Daniel scoots off the bed and stands. "Maybe we need to change that. I'd love to help you decorate it."

He stares down at me, a smile playing at the corners of his mouth.

How can I say no?

"The decorations are in the garage." I smile, and Daniel's lips turn up into a full grin.

He grabs my hand. "Let's go then."

I let him pull me to my feet. We go upstairs, and I don't care that I'm in my pyjamas. I find Mum in the kitchen where the smell of chocolate cake wafts from the oven.

"Jess." She comes to the doorway and gives me a tight hug. "How are you feeling?"

I shrug. "Tired. But Daniel said he'd help me put up the Christmas tree."

"That's a lovely idea." She glances at Daniel then back at me. She's smiling, but it doesn't quite reach her eyes. "When you're done we can have some cake."

"That sounds yum," Daniel says.

"You'll find everything you need in the garage." Mum goes to the kitchen sink. "Left side of the cupboard."

Daniel and I head outside and take the garden path through the yard to our freestanding double garage. We go in through the access door on the side, and I flick the light on. My mum is always so organised, and we find the tree tucked neatly in its original box beside another box labelled 'Xmas Decs'. I carry the tree, and Daniel picks up the decorations. I follow him back inside, taking a moment to check out the way his surf shorts hug his arse.

Stop perving, Jessica.

Our lounge room is quite big and takes up about a third of the top level of the house. Daniel and I go in and set the boxes down.

I stare up at him through a blurry haze of tears. "Everything," I whisper. Then I get to my feet and run downstairs to my room.

"Everything is wrong!" I scream, grabbing the towel that's taped to my wardrobe door. I rip it down and toss it across the room. "You're a murderer," I yell at my reflection. "Why did you do this? Why did you take her from me? I want her back."

I charge the mirror and slap it with my palm. I kick the bottom of it and it cracks, but I don't stop. I hit it again, and again, and again.

"Jess, stop," Daniel says. "You'll hurt yourself."

Hr grabs my shoulders, but I shrug him off.

I slap the mirror again.

The crack spreads, and the glass moves beneath my fingers. It cracks in another place and I stop, staring at my fractured reflection. At the broken pieces of myself.

I give it one last pound with my fist, and a piece of mirror pops out, slicing my hand.

"Aarrrgh!" I cry, and kick the base of the mirror.

"Jess!" Daniel pulls me backwards.

A big piece of glass falls from my wardrobe door and crashes onto the floor. For a moment all I can do is stare at it. My face reflects back at me in a hundred fractured pieces.

Then the tears come.

So many tears.

When will they ever end?

"I can't do this anymore," I say.

My knees crumple, and Daniel catches me before I hit the floor. He lets me down gently and pulls me into

his lap, stroking my hair.

"Shh," he says. "I'm here. It's okay."

I feel like screaming at him that nothing is okay, but all my energy has been used up and cried out with my tears. Daniel snatches the towel from the floor and wraps it around my hand.

"Breathe for a minute, then we'll look at your cut," he says.

"Jess? What was the noise? Were you yelling?" Mum's voice comes from the hallway. "Daniel? What happened?"

"Do you have a first-aid kit?"

"Of course. I'll get it."

Daniel kisses my hair, and I squeeze my eyes closed. Why is he still here? Why is he helping me when he could be with someone normal? Someone who isn't so messed up.

"Do you think you can stand?" Daniel whispers near my ear.

No. But I nod.

"Keep this pressed on your cut." He pushes my good hand on top of the wounded one, then hooks his fingers under my armpits and lifts me up.

My legs are weak, but I manage not to buckle to the floor again.

Mum is in the doorway, looking around us at the destruction in my bedroom.

"Bring her down to the rumpus room," she says. "We can lay her on the daybed."

Daniel walks me down the hallway. When we pass Josephine's room, I touch the closed door with my fingertips. We reach the daybed, and Daniel lays me down on the

foam mattress, propping my head up with a couple of cushions. He sits on the edge and Mum kneels in front of me.

No one talks while she looks at my cut. She swabs it with Dettol and puts a couple of butterfly plasters on it to hold the cut together, then wraps a bandage around my hand.

"It's not too deep. A clean slice, so it should heal quickly. But it might throb for a while," she says, packing up the first-aid supplies.

"I'll put this back." Daniel grabs the box.

"Upstairs, under the sink." Mum smiles at him. She waits until she can hear his footsteps on the top level before speaking again. "Tell me how I can help you, Jess?"

I blink a few times, and concentrate on the sensation of the tear sliding down my cheek. "I'm not sure you can."

Dear Josie

I haven't written to you for a while. Truth is, I don't really want to write about all the stuff that's been happening lately. But Penny said everything I'm feeling, my emotions and stuff, are all healthy.

There's that word again. Healthy.

I don't feel healthy. I feel broken.

Like my bedroom mirror.

Daniel and I were putting up the Christmas tree and it was so great, spending the time with him. I was actually smiling and having a bit of fun. But then I found that ornament we had made for Mum and Dad. You know, the one with our photo in it?

I snapped. I couldn't take it anymore.

I haven't looked at myself in what feels like forever, and when I saw my face next to yours in that photo, it was like something inside of me broke all over again.

The mirror smashed because I hit it until it cracked. Then it fell off the door and shattered all over the floor. I cut myself, but Mum patched me up.

Every time I see my reflection, for a split second I think

you're back. That you didn't really die. And in that minute period of time everything with the world is right again. But then I realise I'm just looking at myself, and it all comes crashing down around me.

Your broken sister, Jess xxx

He misses her, too

Christmas was quiet for Mum, Dad, and me. We spent the day together opening presents, and eating our traditional meal. Mum seemed happy to keep herself busy cooking the ham, preparing the salads, and making Pavlova for desert.

I wish I could have spent some time with Daniel, but he was busy with his own family Christmas. I got to see him a couple of days later though. He gave me a new notebook to write to Josephine in, since I've almost finished my first one. The cover has sunflowers on it, and the fact that he remembered they were Josephine's favourite flower made my heart swell.

Now, it's New Year's Eve, and Stacey is sitting on my bed staring at me.

"Come on, Jess. It's going to be great."

I take a deep breath. "Why do we have to go?"

"Please." She cocks her head to the side and pouts. "Getting out of the house and spending some time with your friends is exactly what you need."

I'm not sure what I need.

"They're Josie's friends."

"Don't be silly. They're yours now, too."

Jarred is going to be at Veronica's party, and I haven't spoken to him since the day Josephine died. When I've seen him, he's had a scowl on his face. And he hasn't exactly tried to talk to me.

But maybe I should go. Doing something normal might stop my parents worrying about me so much.

"Fine," I say.

"Yay." She claps her hands. "But you have to promise me you'll try to at least act like you're having a good time."

Act. Sure, I can do that. My heart drops though, because I remember standing in the disabled toilet at the airport with Josephine, and having her tell me what a great actress she was.

I force a smile, and Stacey and I get ready to head into the city. I go light on the make-up, and slip into a pair of white shorts, a blue floral singlet top, and a pair of thongs, then pack my overnight bag. Mum said she'd drive us to the station, so we go upstairs to find her. A knock sounds on the front door as I walk past. When I open it, Daniel is standing there.

"Hey. You look nice." He smiles, then glances over my shoulder.

I turn to follow his stare.

Stacey leans against the banister, grinning.

My cheeks grow hot, and I suck my bottom lip between my teeth. I'm not sure if I'm embarrassed because of Daniel's words, or because Stacey is staring at us so intently. I glare at her, then look back at Daniel.

"I'll go find your mum," Stacey says.

I wait for her to disappear around the corner before I say, "We're going to Veronica's party."

"I know." Daniel runs a hand through his hair. "Katie's going after she sees Levi. I wanted to tell you to have a great time tonight."

"I'll try." This time I don't have to force my smile.

"If you need me, just call."

"We're sleeping over. I should be right to come home with Stacey tomorrow."

"Maybe we can do something then?"

"I'd like that." I stare at him.

Kiss me.

I lean towards him. I *so* badly want him to kiss me.

He steps forward, and my heart races. It's only been a few seconds since the last words left my mouth, but it feels like hours.

Daniel leans down and presses a chaste kiss to my lips. I place my hands on his chest, and he wraps his arms around me, pulling me close. His lips are warm and soft, and his touch ignites little butterflies in my stomach.

I want every kiss to feel like this.

"Ahem," Stacey clears her throat.

Daniel pulls away. "I'll see you tomorrow," he whispers in my ear. "Happy New Year."

"You, too," I manage to say.

I don't turn around until he's outside and I've closed

the door, but when I do, Stacey and Mum are staring at me. Stacey has a lopsided smile on her face, and Mum's eyebrows are raised. Neither of them say anything though.

Mum drives Stacey and me to the train station, and I'm busting to talk to Stacey about Daniel, but I'm not going to do that in the car in front of Mum. We jump out in the drop off zone. Mum waves as she pulls away.

"Oh my God, he kissed you!" Stacey squeals.

"I know!" I say, happiness bubbling inside me.

"You should be staying home with him." Stacey walks towards the stairs, then stops and stares at me. "No. No. We're going to have a great time tonight. Then you can kiss him some more tomorrow."

I laugh, shaking my head at Stacey's enthusiasm. We reach the top of the stairs and go down to find Veronica and Rachel on the platform, waiting for the train.

"Hey, bitches," Veronica says. "Ready to party?"

Rachel rolls her eyes, and Stacey says, "You bet." She flops onto the bench beside Veronica.

The train pulls in a few minutes later, and we climb on, taking the empty seats in the vestibule area. It's just after lunch, so there aren't many people on the train. We get off at North Sydney station and follow Veronica down the street to the hotel. She checks us in, and we head up to the eleventh floor.

Stacey dumps her bag then runs to the glass door leading to the balcony, sliding it open to go outside. "Look at the view."

It is pretty amazing. I walk to the glass window and gaze out over the harbour. The fireworks are going to look pretty spectacular tonight. I put my bag with Stacey's

and look around the hotel room. There are two bedrooms and a sitting room. Some green shopping bags sit on a table in the corner near the lounge. Underneath it is an esky, I assume filled with drinks for the night.

"Jess, you want to help Rach set up the food? I'm going to get changed." Veronica disappears into the first bedroom.

Rachel unpacks the bags, and I go to stand beside her. She pulls out paper plates, packets of chips, and finger food. Containers filled with carrot and celery sticks. Veronica must have had it dropped off so it was ready for us when we got here. I'm surprised she didn't ask the hotel staff to set it all up.

Rachel and I don't talk while we work. Stacey comes in and grabs some chips. The door opens as she's stuffing a second round in her mouth.

Jarred and Geoff enter the room, and I freeze. Veronica comes out of the bedroom dressed in a sleek cocktail dress and stilettoes. Geoff looks her up and down. Jarred glares at me.

"In the next room," Veronica says. "This way." She toddles over to the boys and herds them to the door leading to the adjoining suite.

I twist my fingers together. Tonight may not go so well if Jarred keeps giving me death stares. Maybe he does wish I was dead. He would probably switch me with Josephine if he had the chance.

"You should eat something," Stacey says, shoving a plate of chips under my nose. "You won't get drunk as fast."

I take a handful of chips then grab some carrot sticks. After a few bites, a sick feeling settles into the pit of my stomach. To try to take my mind off everything, I head

out to the balcony and sit at the small table. It would be nice to be able to completely empty my mind and enjoy the view of the harbour, but thinking about absolutely nothing is impossible. Especially when I have so much to think about.

Stacey plonks into a chair beside me. Rachel comes onto the balcony with a glass of champagne in her hand and leans against the railing. A minute later the boys are out on their balcony. They sit at the table. Jarred glances at me, his brow pinched and his jaw clenched.

Tonight is definitely going to be fun.

"Hello!" Veronica yells from inside our room. "Welcome to party central. Only fun allowed. Chuck your bags in the second bedroom, then come join us on the balcony."

I look over my shoulder as Katie and Karen come into the room. Stacey jumps up, and I follow her inside. Good timing. It means I can get away from Jarred's glare.

"Hey." Katie smiles.

"Yay," Stacey says. "You're finally here."

"Is there a third bedroom?" Katie points to the door the boys went through.

"We have adjoining suites," Veronica says. "Plenty of beds for everyone, although we have to fight over who gets to sleep with the boys."

Karen folds her arms over her chest. "I don't think we'll be fighting."

"I don't think we'll be sleeping." Veronica laughs.

"Tonight is going to be so much fun." Stacey claps her hands, and I love how enthusiastic she is.

Veronica grins. "That's the plan."

I stay quiet. I'm not really feeling the party vibe.

We go back onto the balcony, and Veronica hands out glasses of champagne.

"Don't drink that too fast," Geoff calls out, smirking at Katie.

"I'll make sure I don't," Katie says.

"Wouldn't want you throwing up on anyone." Geoff smirks and takes a swig from his beer.

Katie's brow creases. "How do you … who told you I did that?" She looks around at all of us.

I shrug, because it wasn't me. What happened to Katie at Schoolies isn't my story to tell.

"Word travels," Jarred says.

"It's not like you've never been drunk and done something stupid before," Karen says.

He laughs. "Fair enough."

"Can we just have a good time tonight?" Veronica asks. "Tomorrow is a new year. We can put all the crap from this one behind us."

Stacey raises her glass. "I'll drink to that." She sips her bubbly drink.

"We need music." Veronica goes inside. She comes back with her phone and a small speaker. "What should we listen to?"

"Anything." Rachel sits with her feet up on the railing. "As long as it's loud."

Rachel glances at Katie and sniggers, then takes another sip of her drink. Rachel doesn't like very many people, and I admit that I don't really like her either, but she seems bitchier than usual. Looking at her now, her eyes are sad. I haven't asked her how she's doing since Josephine died.

I haven't asked any of my sister's friends how they are. I've been too caught up in myself to worry about them. Maybe I'm the one who's the bitch.

All the girls get comfortable in chairs on the balcony. Jarred and Geoff stay on their side, drinking their beers. I sit with Stacey and stay quiet, not in the mood for talking. Veronica goes inside and comes back with food, passing it around before turning the music up to a volume that makes talking without shouting impossible. I don't mind. It makes it easier to not think.

For the next few hours I sit and listen to the noises around me, and stare at the lights on the harbour. I don't join in the conversations much, and I watch my friends get tipsy and then a little drunk. I have a couple of glasses of champagne, but start to get a headache, so I stop.

By the time the nine o'clock fireworks come around, Rachel is drunk and giggling. It actually makes me smile, because it's the happiest I've seen her all night. Rachel gets up to go inside, and Katie follows her. When they come back, Katie's jaw is clenched and her brow knitted. Rachel must have said something to her.

Karen and Katie have a quick conversation that I can't hear, but to be honest I don't want to know what they're talking about. I want to watch the sky explode with colour.

"Two minutes," Geoff calls from the other balcony.

Everyone is on their feet and at the railing. With six of us it's pretty squishy. Katie grabs my hand and pulls me inside.

"There's more room next door," she says.

I don't want to go next door to where Jarred is, but I let Katie drag me with her anyway. We go onto the balcony,

and I don't miss Geoff's sideways glance or Jarred's frown. Moments later, the sky explodes in an array of colours.

Katie curls her fingers around the railing and puts her head back. I stand to the side with my arms wrapped around my middle, focusing on the bursts of colour so I don't have to look anywhere else. Each new display burns itself into my retinas, leaving an afterimage that disappears when the next explosion comes.

The bangs ring out like gunshots over the water. The lights shimmer on the surface of the harbour, and the way they move reminds me of how tears look in someone's eyes moments before they spill over.

Geoff leaves the railing and sits at the table. "I hope the midnight show is better than that."

"It always is," I whisper.

Katie leans close to me and gives my shoulder a nudge. "Midnight will be awesome. You know, I've never seen the New Year's fireworks up close."

"It's been a couple of years since I have," I say. "The last time was with Josie. Mum and Dad let us come to the city on our own." A tear escapes onto my cheek and I swipe it away.

"I remember that," Katie says. "I wanted to come with you, but I wasn't allowed."

I take a shuddering breath, and rest my head on Katie's shoulder. "I miss her."

"I know." Katie puts an arm around me.

"It's my fault she's dead."

"Don't be silly. It was an accident," Katie says. "You weren't even there."

"I'm the reason she was out."

Jarred scoffs, but I don't lift my head to look at him. I close my eyes, and feel Katie's head turn, but I don't want to know what looks are being exchanged between them. I just want to get out of here, go home and curl up in bed. Or better still, see Daniel so I can hug him.

"It's still not your fault," Katie says.

A chair scrapes as someone stands. My guess is, Jarred has gone inside.

"The last thing I said to her was …" My breath catches in my throat. "I called her a bitch, Katie." I move away from my friend and press my stomach against the railing, looping my fingers around the cool metal and staring at the lights on the bridge.

"Hey, what're you doing over there?" Karen yells. "Come back. We have more food."

"Hang on," Katie says. She touches me on the elbow. "You didn't mean it. Josie loved you, and she'd hate to see you like this. Let's go eat something. You might feel better with food in your stomach."

I nod, and we go inside. Jarred pushes past Katie back onto the balcony.

Katie looks from Jarred to me. "What's up with him?"

I open my mouth to reply, but then close it again, shaking my head and looking at the boy who seems to be hurting as much as me. "Nothing. Don't worry about it."

"Okay, but you know you can talk to me, yeah?"

I smile with my mouth closed. "Of course."

I follow Katie next door where the other girls are eating pizza.

"More champagne," Rachel yells. She fills her glass then stocks up on pizza slices, taking it all out to the balcony.

Veronica rolls her eyes. "I have a feeling I'll be picking her up off the floor soon." She follows Rachel, pizza in hand.

I grab a napkin and put a slice of pizza on it, even though I'm not hungry. I sit on the couch and get comfy in the corner, drawing my legs up underneath me.

Stacey, Katie, and Karen talk in hushed whispers at the table. They're probably talking about me, but I'm too tired to care about what they're saying. All of them go back to the balcony, and I listen to the chatter of voices in sporadic bursts through the music. I stay on the couch and pick at my pizza.

After a while the door to the adjoining suite opens and Jarred stands in the doorway. He glares at me, and I frown. What does he want? Is he just going to stand there and try to hurt me with his eyes? I draw my knees to my chest and hug them.

He goes back into his room, and I sit here confused. Does he want to talk to me? Why doesn't he just come over and say something?

I get to my feet and go to the door, peering into Jarred and Geoff's suite. Jarred is standing in the middle of the room, hands in his pockets and his back to me. Geoff is on the balcony. I walk in, then pull the door to and move around Jarred until I'm in front of him, face to face.

"Why do you keep glaring at me?" I ask.

He moves his gaze from the city outside until it's fixed on me. "Because you don't deserve to have me look at you any other way."

"I know it's my fault." I tuck my hair behind my ear and stare at my feet. "You have no idea what I'm going through."

"What?" Jarred spits. "You think I don't know how much this hurts?"

"How could you?" I look up at him again. "She was my sister."

"And I loved her."

"You broke up with her," I yell.

The music blares. The others talk loudly on the balcony next door, but I can't make out what they're saying. Hopefully they can't hear us either.

"Ten seconds," someone yells.

"What you did was a low move," Jarred says. "You deserve everything you get."

Voices chant the countdown to New Year. *Five, four, three ...*

The door behind Jarred opens and Katie steps into the room, her pretty face marred with a questioning frown. Outside, fireworks explode to cheers of 'Happy New Year'.

"I'm sorry," I say as tears course down my cheeks.

"Tell that to your dead sister," he says.

"I thought you knew it was me."

"I did, eventually, but ..." Jarred puts a hand in his hair and pulls. "I expected you to stop."

"Then how can you blame me if you knew?" I step towards him, my hot tears coming faster.

"Because you're the one who agreed to the dare," Jarred yells.

Karen rushes into the room. "Katie? You missed the countdown. What's going on?"

I drag my gaze away from Jarred and look at Katie, swiping the tears off my cheeks. She comes into the room

in big strides, her face screwed up in anger.

"I can't believe you're still playing that game!" she shouts. "What happened, Jess?"

I close my eyes, and my shoulders shake as the tears come. There's movement around me, but I don't want to see what's going on. I just want to curl up in a ball and have this all go away.

When I open my eyes again, Geoff has come inside and Jarred has his back to me.

"Josie should never have been in that car." He snatches his keys from the coffee table, making a line for the door.

"Jarred, stop," Katie says.

I hug myself and rub my arms. A chill runs through me, even though I'm not cold.

"What?" he asks.

"Don't drive," Katie says. "Don't … don't drink and drive."

Jarred picks up his backpack and nods, but doesn't say anything, then leaves. I grip my upper arms to try to stop them shaking. Geoff rubs his face, then in a burst of anger that makes me flinch, he punches the wall, leaving behind a red mark on the concrete.

"This is so fucked up." He grabs his bag, following Jarred.

"What's happening in here?" Stacey stands in the doorway leading to the other suite.

"I have no idea." Karen throws her hands up then flops onto the couch.

"Jess?" Stacey comes towards me, her eyebrows raised. "What happened?"

The shaking in my shoulders gets worse, and I suck in a deep breath, staring at my shoes. "Can we go home?

I can't do this anymore." My legs give way and I kneel on the floor, lying down and pulling my knees to my chest.

"How about we get you to bed." Stacey touches my shoulder. "The boys are gone so we can sleep in here. Tomorrow will be better, I promise. And we can go home first thing." My best friend helps me to my feet, and we move towards the bedrooms. "We'll see you all in the morning," she says to Katie and Karen.

Stacey closes the bedroom door, then pulls back the covers on the bed and helps me climb in. I'm still dressed, and I could do with a toothbrush, but I don't care. I don't have the energy to do anything but lie here and try to forget about everything.

I roll onto my side. Stacey lies beside me and plays with my hair. I close my eyes, and concentrate on the feeling of her fingers running through the strands. It's soothing, and it helps me calm down.

"Want to talk about it?" Stacey asks. "We haven't really discussed anything that happened that day."

"No. Yes. I don't know," I say, keeping my eyes closed.

"I know you and Josie twin swapped," she says, still twirling my hair. "I haven't said anything to you, because of everything that's happened. I figured you'd talk to me when you were ready."

I slip my hand into hers and give it a gentle squeeze. I haven't told Stacey about Jarred, or about what Josephine and I did. There just never seemed a time right enough to talk to her about it. She's my best friend, and I've completely shut her out.

"How did you know it was Josie?" I ask, opening my eyes to look at her.

"Are you kidding?" Stacey puts her free hand under her cheek. "I knew the minute you two walked out of the bathroom at the airport. I didn't say anything because I figured you both had your reasons. And it was fun spending some time with Josie. I let her squirm for a bit, but I told her I knew who she was before we landed in Sydney."

"I think she was trying to get some distance from Jarred," I say. "They slept together while we were away, and I think she freaked out."

Stacey is quiet. She presses her lips together. "She told me," she finally says. "She told me a lot of things."

"Like what?"

"Stuff about her friends. She was tired of them. She said she needed a break for a few hours. She made me promise I'd go along with it, and pretend I didn't know it was her."

I'm not sure if I feel hurt that my sister didn't talk to me about any of this, or if I'm sad because I didn't notice anything was wrong. I let go of Stacey's hand and tuck mine under my cheek, mirroring her. I think back to that day at the airport when I asked Josephine if she was okay, and she said she was. All she wanted was to have some fun. I should have pushed her more to talk to me.

"Josie would never have had that accident if it wasn't for me," I say, trying to find an in to talk to Stacey about Jarred.

"That's not true, Jess."

"Just ... let me finish. There's more to the story." I take a deep breath. "I did my best to pretend I was her. I didn't like the idea of swapping, but she said that's what she wanted, so I went along with it. I knew something was

wrong, but she said she was fine. I figured we could talk about it when we got home. She told me if Jarred tried to do anything, to just … push him away, because she did it all the time." I take another deep breath. "I thought Jarred would figure it out pretty quickly, but he didn't until I made him look at me. By then …"

"Oh no, Jess." Stacey lifts her head from the pillow. "What happened?"

"He kissed me, and I should have stopped him, because he was my sister's boyfriend, and I should have told him before it went that far, but … I liked it. And I kissed him back." I stop and wait for Stacey to say something, but she doesn't. "I'm a terrible person."

"No. You're not. You're one of the sweetest, and kindest, people I know."

"Doesn't change what I did."

"But it's not your fault, Jess." Stacey's fingers slide through my hair again. "You can't place all of the blame on yourself."

"We twin swapped, and I kissed Jarred, and Josie and I had a huge fight, then he broke up with her, and Josie … died. If I didn't do what I did, Jarred would never have done what he did, we would never have fought with her, and she'd still be alive."

"You don't know that for sure. Josie and Levi … It was just the wrong place at the wrong time," Stacey says. "And I'm sure Levi is going to be gutted when he finally wakes up and finds out what happened. Have you been to see him?"

"No," I reply. "I don't blame him for what happened, but I'm not sure I'll cope with seeing him … hurt."

"It might be good for you. And it might be good for Katie to know you support her."

Until now, I've managed to talk and not cry, but my eyes are hot and I have a headache from holding the tears back. My shoulders are tense and I try to relax them, but when I do a gut-wrenching sob explodes from my mouth. Tears fall from my eyes and run over the bridge of my nose.

Stacey drapes an arm over me and holds me tight. "It's obvious Jarred is hurting, too. And I think it's time you have a good talk to him about all of this. He's dealing with losing his girlfriend, and almost losing his best friend. He's probably not himself right now."

"He can't even look at me ... I don't blame him. *I* can't look at myself."

"Maybe he finds it hard to be around you because ... he misses her, too."

Dear Josie

Tonight was a disaster. It's New Year's Eve—well, New Year's Day now, but it's really early—and I had hoped to be able to relax a little, have some fun with my friends, but everything ended up shit and crap and so fucked up.

I think I forgot to tell you.

Veronica invited me to a party.

She invited Stacey, and Karen, and Katie, too. We're in the city. Her dad booked her two hotel rooms with views of the bridge and the harbour.

I thought it would be good.

It wasn't.

I snuck out of bed to write to you so I wouldn't wake Stacey.

I have to tell you what happened.

Jarred is the reason everything went to shit. We haven't spoken about what happened, and he's been more than hostile to me. He's been a right royal dick. Only I'm too guilt ridden and weak to really stand up to him. Or say anything in my defence that would make any sense.

None of this makes any sense!

We had an argument and he stormed out. He told me I deserve everything I get.

Do I?

Do I deserve to suffer like this for the rest of my life?

Will there be a day when I won't feel like I do now?

I told Stacey everything. And I'm here writing this now because I haven't told you everything. I never had a chance to talk to you properly about this because you died. So I guess I should talk to you about it now.

Yes, I kissed Jarred, and yes, I liked it.

I should never have done that. I should have been strong enough to push him away and tell him the truth. But you were so adamant that you wanted us to do the swap, and I was just going along with what you wanted. I told you I didn't want to do it.

I just read over that last part, and look at me making excuses to justify what I did to you. I'm so sorry, Josie. If I could, I would go back to that moment in the airport, and tell you no. And I would get you to talk to me and tell me what was bothering you. Because I knew there was something wrong, and I was going to talk to you about it when we got home.

I never had the chance.

I want all the chances with you again, but I know I can't have them.

And now, I'll never know what you were dealing with or going through. No one will know. You're not here to tell us, to tell me. And knowing something was wrong but I didn't help, is tearing me apart.

Stacey thinks I need to talk to Jarred. Really talk to him.

I don't know what was going on between you and him.

The Other Side of Me

I'm so confused about all of this, and I can't imagine what you were thinking or feeling about anything. I've tried to get inside your head and think like you, but to me you always seemed so perfectly happy.

Were you actually unhappy, and I didn't even notice?

I guess now I'll never know.

Your tortured sister, Jess xxx

Losing myself

My sleep is restless, and I wake several times before dawn. It gets to the point where I don't want to wake Stacey, so I slip out of bed and go to sit on the balcony. I slouch in my chair, resting my feet on the railing. The early morning is quiet, and the water on the harbour is still. I watch the bobbing boats and wait for the sun to peek over the horizon.

"You couldn't sleep either?" Katie moves a chair on her balcony so it's close to the end nearest me.

I shake my head. "I don't sleep well these days."

Katie is quiet for a few heartbeats. "Do you want to talk about anything?"

I look over at her, knowing she wants to help, but I poured everything out to Stacey last night. I can't do it again just yet.

"I'm not sure I can get the words out and make any sense." I pause, and let my eyes unfocus. "None of it makes any sense."

"Maybe you should write it down. I find writing in my journal helps with a lot of stuff."

I look away from Katie towards the bridge. I have been writing stuff down, but I'm at the point where I'm questioning if it's helping. "Maybe," I reply.

Katie and I sit and watch the sun come up, throwing its rays across the water and making it sparkle. For a second I marvel at the beauty of it, then the thought of Josephine not being able to see something so beautiful makes me sad again.

"Every day is a fresh start," Katie says. "It has to be better than the last one, right?"

Daniel told me the same thing. It must be a Sullivan family mantra. I don't say anything back, because so far all my days have been the same. They haven't felt like starting over at all. Just the one continuous nightmare. My sister is still dead. How can tomorrow be better than today if Josephine is never going to be here again?

"Who wants to go home?" Karen comes onto Katie's balcony and stands behind her, stretching.

"I think home sounds fantastic." Katie jumps up and pushes her chair in under the table. "Want to train it with us?" She looks over at me.

I nod. "I'll have a shower, and see what Stacey's doing."

When I go back into the bedroom, Stacey rolls over and groans. She grabs her pillow and puts it over her face.

"I don't want to get up." Her voice is muffled under the pillow.

I chuckle and head for the shower, standing there for a good ten minutes and letting the hot water run over me. I convince Stacey to get out of bed and shower, too. Then we gather our stuff and help Veronica tidy the two suites before saying goodbye to her and Rachel and walking to the station.

The train trip home is quiet, and the four of us don't talk much. Stacey and I part ways with Katie and Karen as they walk up the highway towards Karen's place. I call Mum and she comes to pick us up.

"Did you have a good night, girls?" Mum asks.

"It was great," Stacey says from the back seat.

I smile at Mum and nod my agreement. "But I'm tired."

We drop Stacey off at her place on the way home, and a few seconds after she's out of the car my phone buzzes with a message.

Stacey: Call me if U want 2 talk

Me: Thanks

I press the button on the side of my phone and the screen goes black. Out the window I watch the main strip go by as we enter our street. We pass Levi's house, and the driveway is empty. Of course his car isn't there. It was written off in the accident. I should ask Katie again how he's going.

"Do you want to go and visit Levi?" Mum asks, as we pull into our driveway.

"What? Why would you think that?"

"It might be a nice thing to do." Mum turns the car off and puts the handbrake on. "It wasn't his fault, Jess. He will need his friends' support."

I frown and think about what she said. Should I go

and see him? Can I handle something like that? I don't blame him, I blame myself. But what if seeing him breaks me all over again?

"I'll ask Daniel to take me," I say, then get out of the car.

Mum follows me to the front door. "I can drive you if you like."

I use my key to get in. "It's okay. Daniel might want to see him, too."

I race downstairs to my room and dump my bag, sitting on the bed and pulling up my messages.

Me: Hey. Good night?

Daniel: Would've been better with U

Me: Are U busy?

Daniel: Nope. Happy New Year

Me: ♥ Can U take me 2 hospital?

Daniel: Sure. When?

Me: Now?

Daniel: Give me 10

While I wait, I run a brush through my hair, and moisturise my face again. I pace my room, thinking about what to say to Levi, even though he probably won't be able to hear me. I don't think he's awake yet. What am I doing? Should I go? How will his mum react?

A knock sounds on the front door and I grab my purse, racing up the stairs.

"Bye, Mum." I yank the door open and barrel into Daniel. "Let's go before I chicken out." I stride up the driveway and jump into his mum's car.

"Where's the fire?" Daniel asks as he slips into the driver's seat.

"I just ..." I stop and look at him, gathering my thoughts.

"I want to see Levi."

"What brought this on?" Daniel starts the car and reverses onto the road.

Guilt. I shrug, because I can't fully explain it to him, and I don't want to say anything because he might talk me out of it. I smile and pretend to be okay.

I *am* okay.

If I tell myself enough times it might come true.

I can be okay.

We drive to the hospital without talking much. I turn the radio up so it's hard to say anything. Right now, I don't want to talk. I did enough talking last night. All I want is to sit and tell myself everything is okay.

I'm okay.

Daniel parks the car. "You ready to go in?"

I blow a breath out between my teeth. "I have to tell you something first. I've been seeing a grief counsellor. Mum booked me into a psychologist not long after Josie died, and I've been seeing a counsellor ever since. Her name is Penny. She thinks doing things like this, seeing Levi, will help."

"Whatever works," Daniel says, and I love that he doesn't question or judge.

We get out of the car, and Daniel leads me to the ICU main door where he picks up the phone on the wall.

"Is Yvonne White there please?" he asks. He points to the small basin on the wall and gestures for me to wash my hands. I do, and then Daniel says into the phone, "Hi, it's Daniel. I'm here with Jess. Is it all right if we come in?"

A moment later he hangs up, and there's a click from

the door. It opens, and we go inside. I follow Daniel through the ward, trying not to look at the sick people. Sick people in every room. What a depressing place.

Daniel stops at room seven. "Hi, Yvonne."

She turns away from the monitoring window, and I catch a glimpse of Levi over her shoulder.

"Daniel, Jess. So nice to see you both." She comes and hugs me, and at first I'm not sure what to do. I hug her back then she holds me at arm's length. "How are you doing?"

I force a smile, and it feels like a grimace. "Okay."

There's that word again.

I am okay.

"Do you want to go in?" Daniel asks, touching my elbow.

I stare at Levi through the glass. He's hooked up to several machines with wires and tubes running all over the place. I nod and try to swallow. It hurts because my mouth is dry. Daniel opens the door for me. I walk up to the bed and stand at the railing. Daniel stays close to my side.

"I'm so sorry," I whisper, looking down at Levi. How has Katie been able to come here and see him every day? He looks as broken as I feel. "You're here because of me." I sob. "You wouldn't be here if it wasn't for me."

"He's going to be all right, Jess." Daniel puts an arm around my shoulders, but I shrug him off.

This is not okay.

I am NOT okay.

"It's all my fault," I scream.

"Jess, honey, calm down." Yvonne is at my side.

"You don't understand," I yell. Hot tears run tracks

down my cheeks. "It's my fault. I killed my sister. I killed her." I twist my hands into my hair and pull, relishing the pain in my scalp. I open my mouth and let out a cry so deep it feels like it rips my soul from my chest.

"Shh," Yvonne whispers. "Come on."

She grabs my wrists and gently pulls them away from my head. I let her, and she hugs me. I fold my arms up between us and cry into her shoulder, letting her rub my back. Then Daniel presses his hands to my upper arms and turns me around, hugging me to him and leading me away from Levi's bedside.

"Levi!" someone yells from outside the room.

I lift my head from Daniel's shoulder and stare at Katie. She's standing at the window, her eyes wide.

"Katie?" Levi's voice is raspy. "Mum ...? Where am I?"

Katie stumbles into the room, tears streaming down her face. A nurse pushes past her, then a doctor and another nurse are in the room. It suddenly feels crowded, and my chest tightens.

"Everyone, out," one of the nurses says. "There are too many people in here." She stands between Katie and the bed, stopping her from going any closer.

Daniel pulls me towards Katie and the door. "Levi, I'm sorry," I sob. "It's my fault. It should've been me ... My fault ... Josie ..." Daniel takes me out of the room.

A minute later Katie is in the hall with us, her eyes red and puffy. She goes to the window and stares at Levi through the glass. Another sob makes my chest ache, and Katie looks at me over her shoulder.

"Come on, Jess." Daniel hugs me close, resting his chin on the top of my head. "I'll take you home."

I let him lead me back to the car, stumbling along the way because I can't see through the blur of my tears. Daniel puts me into the front passenger seat and straps my seatbelt around me. He doesn't try to talk to me, or tell me everything is all right. He just kisses my forehead and closes the door, then drops into the driver's seat and takes us towards home.

On the way I rest my forehead against the window and close my eyes, concentrating on the rocking movement of the car as we make all the turns leading to our street. Daniel turns into his driveway and kills the engine. I don't move. I'm not sure I have enough energy to. I sense him looking at me.

"Can you wait here? I need to go talk to Mum."

I nod my reply, keeping my eyes closed. Then I hear him open the door and get out.

A few minutes later, my door opens and I sit up so I don't fall out of the car. Daniel reaches in and unbuckles my seatbelt, helping me up. My knees are weak, and I'm exhausted. My house is only a few doors up the street, but the walk home seems impossible. All I feel like doing is curling up right here on the ground and crying until I fall asleep.

Daniel takes me into his arms and helps me walk to my house. I give him my keys and he lets us in, taking me downstairs to my room. I sink onto the bed and lie on my side. Daniel stands in the doorway, his hands in his pockets.

"How do I help you, Jess?" he asks, his voice almost a whisper. "How do I prove to you that none of this is your fault?"

"You can't," I say, my throat dry and sore.

He comes and perches on the edge of the bed so his side presses into my stomach. "Can I show you something?"

I adjust my head on the pillow and look up at him. "I guess."

"It requires you to get up and come into Josie's room."

I stare at him for a really long moment. Why does he want me to go into Josephine's room? Especially now.

"Why?" I whisper.

"Do you trust me?"

"I want to trust you."

"Come on." He takes my hand, helps me up, and I follow him down the hall to Josephine's door.

I press my hand against it, knowing that when I open it she won't be there. I want her to be there. Daniel turns the knob and the door swings inwards. We walk in and I rub my arms, hugging myself. Daniel takes my shoulders, turning me towards the mirror on the wardrobe door. Identical to the one that used to be on my door.

I tense and look at my feet.

Daniel's chest presses into my back. He wraps one arm around me, and reaches to lift my chin with his free hand. I squeeze my eyes closed.

"Open your eyes, Jess. What do you see?" he asks.

My eyelids flutter as I fight to keep them closed. Then I open them and stare at my reflection.

"I see Josie."

Daniel rests his cheek against the side of my head. "I see you."

"Every time I look at myself all I see is her."

"Then you're not looking hard enough."

I turn around, away from the mirror, and hide my face against Daniel's chest. "Please. I don't want to look anymore."

"Okay, but there's something else I think you should do. Come on."

He takes my hand and we go back to my bedroom. Daniel picks up the shoebox from my desk and sets it on the bed. He sits in the desk chair and looks at me. I don't make eye contact with him, I just stare at the box with its contents pushing the lid off.

"You are not your sister, Jess," Daniel says. "People look at you, and they see *you*. They don't see Josie. Everyone cares about you so much. You just need to let them in."

I finally look at Daniel, and there are tears in his eyes.

"Why are you crying?" I bite my lip to hold back my own tears.

"Because *I* see *you*. Not Josie. And you're beautiful."

We stare at each other for a moment, and my heart swells. I take a breath to steady myself then sit on the bed with my legs crossed. Carefully, I take the lid off the box. Daniel wheels the chair to the edge of the bed, leaning towards me with his elbows on his knees.

A few notes and a photograph slide off the top of the pile contained by the box. I pick up the picture. It's of Josephine, Rachel, Veronica, Katie, Karen, Stacey, and me. I remember Geoff taking it at the airport, minutes before Josephine and I went into the bathroom. And this time when I look at myself, I see me. Not my sister. We might be identical twins, but now I see how different and unique we really are. I run my finger over Josephine's face.

"I need a mirror," I say. Daniel glances around the room. "Top drawer in the desk." I point without taking my eyes from the photograph.

Daniel opens the drawer and rummages around, then presses a small compact mirror into my hand. I flip it open, and look from my reflection to the photograph, then back again. This time when the tears come, they're happy tears, because in the mirror I see myself. The girl I see has the same eyes and the same hair as the me in the picture.

Identical but not the same.

I smile, and this time it isn't forced. When I look at this photo I remember how exhausted we all were from a week away, but I also remember how I felt. Happy. I was happy in this photo. So maybe I need to find more ways to remember how happy feels. If I can do that, eventually feeling happy might come easier. When I look in the mirror I will always be reminded of my sister, but now I will only see myself.

I place the photo on the bed, then sift through the box. There are so many things inside, some of them damaged by the weather, but one particular envelope catches my eye. There isn't anything remarkable about it in relation to some of the other stuff, like paper flowers and colourful poems. But it's addressed to Josephine and Jessica, written in a scratchy backwards-sloping script.

"Why is my name on this one?" I look up at Daniel.

"Maybe someone has something to say to you, too?" He's been so quiet and patient through all of this.

I turn the envelope over. "Maybe."

"Who do you think it's from?"

I shrug. "I have no idea."

"Open it." Daniel smiles and sits back in the chair.

The envelope is thin, so whatever is inside mustn't be very long. I slip my finger under the edge of the flap and hesitate before tearing it open. If Josephine was here I wouldn't be doing this without her, but she isn't, so I am.

Inside is a single sheet of paper slightly smaller than the envelope. Written on one side is a list.

I hate you because you look the same.
I hate you because you made me feel something.
I hate you because every time I look at you I see her.
I hate you because it's easier than not hating you.
I hate you because you left.
Jarred

Jarred? There's so much pain in his words. I feel it as intensely as my own pain over Josephine's death. Hate is such a strong word, and I take a deep breath as I run my fingers over the ink pressed into the paper. Is he talking to both of us? I turn the note over and there are two lists on the other side—one with *Josephine* at the top, and the other *Jessica.*

Josephine
I hate you because you look like Jessica.
I hate you because you made me feel betrayed.
I hate you because every time I think of you I think of Jessica.
I hate you because loving you is really hard.
I hate you because you died.

Jessica
I hate you because you look like Josephine.
I hate you because you made me feel incredible.
I hate you because every time I look at you, you remind
me of Josephine.
I hate you because I can't love you.
I hate you because she died.

Moments ago I had felt so happy, comfortable with being able to look at myself again and not see my sister. But Jarred's words have opened another wound in my heart, and I understand why he's been acting terribly towards me. I stuff the piece of paper back inside the envelope and wipe a tear from the corner of my eye.

"What did it say?" Daniel asks.

"Can I show you later? I need to see someone first."

He searches my face. "Okay. Who?"

"Jarred." I hold his stare. "What I did got everyone into this mess. I need to make sure he's all right."

"And I need to make sure you are. I'll drive you there tomorrow."

"Thank you."

Daniel stands from the chair and moves the box so he can sit beside me on the bed. He searches my face again, and I lean towards him. He reaches up and caresses my cheek, then he kisses me, and everything falls away.

What I felt for Jarred when he kissed me was nothing compared to what I felt when Daniel pressed his lips to mine for the first time. Jarred gave me butterflies, but Daniel makes my head spin until I'm dizzy.

How can I be so lucky to have someone like Daniel in

my life? Someone willing to do anything for me. I don't know if I deserve him, but I do know that all this time, Daniel has been here, and he is the only thing keeping me from losing myself.

Dear Josie

I went to the hospital to see Levi today. It didn't really go so well. When I saw him, I felt another big ball of guilt slam me in the gut. He's in that hospital bed because of me.

Daniel has been sticking by me through all of this. Through all my outbursts and moments of vulnerability. He really helped me today to see things differently. When we got home from the hospital he took me into your room. It's the only room in the house where the mirror isn't covered. But we keep the door closed anyway.

So, we were in your room, and he got me to look in the mirror, which was really hard, and he asked me what I saw.

I saw you.

Since you died, every time I've looked at myself I've seen you, and it's been so painful.

But Daniel told me what he saw.

He saw me.

I wasn't comfortable standing there, looking at … us, so we went back to my room. This is so exhausting. Writing this all down, telling you about everything, so, so exhausting. I wish you were here so I can just tell you stuff.

Anyway, back in my room Daniel told me I should finally look through the box of letters and things everyone has been leaving you. I've been avoiding it, because I thought all those memories would be too painful. But I think I was wrong.

Daniel told me that when people look at me, they see me, not you. And he started crying. He said he thinks I'm beautiful.

I had the feeling that with him there, I could cope with anything, so I opened the box and took a look at what was inside. I found the photo Geoff took of all us girls at the airport before we switched. And when I looked at that photo I finally realised something.

We may be identical, but we're not the same.

I saw you, and I saw me. I saw us. And that photo, it did something else. Instead of remembering that you died, I remembered how I felt that day. How I was exhausted after a week away with my friends, and how we'd had such a great time. That photo gave me a happy memory, and I know this is still going to be really, really hard, but I hope that the more I look at you, the more happy memories I'll get to keep.

I found something else in the box, too. It was from Jarred. But I'm too tired to write about him tonight. I'm going to go and see him tomorrow. We have a few things we need to discuss. I'll make sure I tell you all about it tomorrow.

Your healing sister, Jess xxx

Smile

After reading Jarred's letter, I spent a little more time with Daniel, going through the contents of the box. So many letters to Josephine, all saying the same thing but in different ways. We love you, we miss you, we wish you were still here.

I think all of those things every second of every minute. All. The. Time.

My sleep was fitful again. I couldn't stop thinking about what I'm going to say to Jarred, and I spent half the night awake worrying over it. I've also spent the entire morning doing the same thing. Worrying.

Now, Daniel is driving me to Jarred's place. I haven't called or texted him, because I'm scared he won't want to see me. Cue more worrying.

"Ring me and I'll come get you," Daniel says.

I have the car door open with one foot out. "I don't know how long I'll be."

"I need to grab some stuff for Mum, so I'll be over at the shops. Take all the time you need."

"Thank you." I lean across the centre console and give him a quick kiss before getting out and closing the door.

"Wave if he's home," Daniel says through his open window.

I give him a thumbs-up and walk up the driveway to the front door. The last time I was here my sister was still alive, and the memory of being here with Jarred hits me in the gut. What am I doing? How is he going to respond to me turning up on his doorstep? I raise my hand to knock, hesitate, then grasp the brass ring of the doorknocker and whack it against the door three times.

Moments later the door opens.

Jarred stands on the other side of the threshold, his brow creased.

"Can we talk?" I ask, before I lose my nerve and run back to the car.

Jarred leans to the side and looks over my shoulder. I turn and wave to Daniel. He raises his hand then pulls away from the kerb.

"Your getaway car just left," Jarred says.

I stare at him for a moment. "I don't want to get away from you."

"What do you want, Jess?"

I reach into the back pocket of my shorts and pull out Jarred's note. "I read your ... list."

"I went back to get that the day after I left it, but it was gone. I figured you read it ages ago."

I shake my head. "I hadn't read any of the notes from the accident site until yesterday."

Jarred leans against the door jamb. "I guess you can come in."

"I thought maybe we could sit in the sun?" I glance around his huge front garden. "It's a beautiful day."

He presses his lips together and comes outside, pulling the door closed behind him. I follow him along a path that runs parallel to the front of the house then branches off into the garden. It takes us to a circle with a small fountain in the middle. There's a garden seat at the head of the circle. Jarred sits on one end and I perch at the other.

I grip the note in my hands and stare at it. "I'm sorry—"

"You've already told me that."

"But I'm sorry for a lot of things." I tilt my head and stare into his eyes. What I want to say to him, I need to say fast, so I can get it out. "I'm sorry that I look like her. I'm sorry that I made you feel what you felt. I'm sorry that every time you look at me you see Josie." I stop because my voice trembles, but Jarred doesn't interrupt. "I'm sorry that you hate me, and I'm sorry … that Josie died."

My eyes blur with tears. I blink them away, making them run down my cheeks. I look at my hands again, and a tear drops from my chin onto Jarred's note, forming a circle with ragged edges.

Jarred doesn't speak.

"Every day I think I might feel a little better," I continue. "You know, that I might get a little better, but it seems like every new day is harder than the last one." I look up at him. "Maybe it doesn't have to be. Maybe we can help each other get through this. Maybe *I* need help getting

through this."

Jarred leans forward and puts his face in his hands. His shoulders shake as he takes a big, heaving breath.

"I miss her," Jarred says through his fingers. "And every time I look at you, it reminds me of how much I loved and hated her all at the same time." He sits back and rubs his knees with his hands. His eyes are red. "When we … when I kissed you, I felt a spark I never felt with Josie. And I thought something had changed. That she all of a sudden was into me more or something. I knew something wasn't right, but I liked how she … you … made me feel. And then you told me what deep down I already knew. That you weren't Josie."

Jarred's words hang between us, and he looks away from me into the garden at the manicured rose bushes with their bright pink flowers. "I guess I felt guilty for having feelings like that for my girlfriend's sister, and that I didn't have them for my actual girlfriend." He looks back at me, and his eyes are haunted with sorrow. "I'm sorry I said it should have been you. It shouldn't have been either of you."

I fiddle with the edges of the note in my hand. "What happened … it's not fair in so many ways. Josie should never have asked me to switch with her. I should've told you straight away I wasn't her, but … I liked kissing you, too."

"So where does that leave us?" Jarred's eyes sparkle with more tears.

I tuck my hair behind my ear, and it's my turn to look away. While Jarred is doing an okay job of holding back his tears, I suck at it. I try to blink them away again, but

it doesn't work. They spill over and my vision blurs.

"We can't," I choke out. "It would be too painful."

Jarred moves along the bench until he's beside me. He puts his arms around me, pulling me close until my forehead fits into the curve of his neck.

I cry.

I let everything out in huge waves of grief and pain, wetting his skin with my tears, and gripping his arm as if he's the only thing that will stop me from falling into the darkest pit of despair.

Jarred puts a hand on my head and strokes my hair. "Maybe ... we can be friends?"

I pull back, and he loosens his embrace. "I'd like that."

Jarred's lips curl up slightly, and he moves away from me a little. "So ... Daniel Sullivan, hey?"

I spurt a laugh and rub my face, clearing the tears from my cheeks. "Um ... yeah. He's helped me a lot recently."

"Does Katie know?"

"She knows, and she seems okay with it."

Jarred folds his arms. "Is it serious?"

"You don't get to ask me that." I swat him on the arm and we both smile. "But I think it is."

"That's really great, Jess." Jarred's tone borders on uncomfortable. He nods and looks at his hands.

"This isn't going to be easy," I say. "But we can try to help each other. How's Levi?"

"He'll make a full recovery."

"That's really good news."

Jarred nods again, and we sit and chat for a while about everything and nothing. We reminisce about some of the good times, the funny times, and the not-so-great.

He tells me about the garden and the seat we're sitting on, how it was put here as a memorial when his grandfather passed away a few years ago, and how he used to sit here with Josephine and talk, like we are now.

"I should probably get home," I finally say. "Daniel will be wondering ..."

"Don't do that," Jarred says. "Don't feel like you can't talk about him. He's important to you, so talk about him. Screw what anyone else thinks. Even me."

"But I care what you think."

"Well, I think that you, of all people, Jessica Hart, deserve to be happy."

"Don't make me cry ... again." I blink and wave a hand in front of my face. "I'm so sick of crying."

I stand and take my phone from my back pocket, sending Daniel a quick text.

Me: Ready when UR

Daniel: B right there

Jarred walks me back through the garden and up the driveway to the road. He stands with his toes hanging off the edge of the kerb, shoving his hands into the pockets of his shorts.

"Did you get into the uni course you wanted?" I ask while we wait.

"Yeah. I'm going to do a degree in business. Follow in Dad's footsteps and all that. You?"

"I haven't decided what to do yet. I'm thinking about deferring for a year like Josie and I originally planned." I shrug. "But I don't want to travel without her. So, I'm really not sure. I got into Newcastle for a communications degree though."

A car engine rumbles in the distance, and I glance up the street. Daniel is driving towards us. I step onto the grass so he can pull into the driveway, then he rolls his window down.

"We all good?" Daniel asks.

I glance at Jarred then back at Daniel. "Yeah, I think so."

Jarred smiles, and I move towards him with my arms out, hoping he'll take the hug. He wraps his arms around me tightly, and I do the same to him.

"See you around, Hart," Jarred says as I pull away.

I walk around the front of the car and get into the passenger seat. "Don't be a stranger," I call through Daniel's open window.

We pull out onto the street and Jarred waves as we pass, heading towards the freeway and home.

"How did it go?" Daniel asks.

"Good," I say. "We cleared a few things up."

"Anything I need to worry about?"

"No, don't be silly." I smile at him. "We're good. But there's one more thing I'd like you to help me with."

"Anything, just name it." Daniel grips the steering wheel and stares at the road ahead.

I take a breath and let it out slowly, because once I ask for this he's not going to let me back out.

"Can you take me to the accident site? I want ... to go back."

Daniel turns his head and glances at me quickly before looking at the road again. "I've been waiting for you to ask."

I settle into my seat for the rest of the drive, unsure if my stomach is rolling because I'm happy or terrified.

I'm probably both.

We turn off the freeway onto the highway. In less than three minutes I'll be facing the place where my sister died. The place where the worst memory of my life was created. I push the image of the car crash from my mind, and sit forward slightly in my seat, gripping the front of it with both hands.

Daniel makes another turn, and the telegraph pole comes into view up ahead. Bursts of colour stick out from the rigid pole. Flowers left for Josephine.

My fingers cramp from gripping the seat so tightly, and my stomach churns as we draw closer. Daniel stops at the stop sign before passing through the intersection and pulling over to the kerb on the other side.

The pole is behind us now, and I'm not sure if I can make myself get out of the car.

"We going to do this?" Daniel asks.

"You might need to help me." I look at him, still gripping the seat.

He gets out and comes around to my door, opening it wide. I release my vice grip on the seat and unbuckle my seatbelt, swinging my legs out of the car and putting my feet flat on the footpath.

"Give me a second," I say. "I just need to sit."

"Take a deep breath."

After a few heartbeats, Daniel holds my hand and pulls me up.

I turn and face the telegraph pole, clutching Daniel's hand. He pushes my door closed, and together we walk to the corner, stopping a couple of metres away. I stare at the cross. It's white with an oval in the centre which holds a photograph of Josephine. Her name is etched into the wood below the picture.

I edge forward and place my feet carefully so I don't step on any of the flowers at the base of the pole. Mum has pinned a couple of plastic sleeves to the wood for people to leave their messages. I'm close enough now to touch the cross. I reach out, my fingers trembling, and run my finger around the edge of the frame that holds Josephine's photo. She smiles back at me, frozen in time and in my memory. I press my palm against the cross and cry, my shoulders shaking as I take big, heaving breaths.

Daniel comes up behind me and puts his hands on my shoulders. I turn into him and he wraps me up in his arms, letting me cry there on the street corner with people walking past and cars driving by.

"Do you want to collect what's here today?" he asks.

I nod and break away from him, turning back to the pole and rubbing my eyes to clear them. I reach into the first sleeve and pull out a bundle of notes and letters, and a handmade accordion card.

I pass the notes and letters to Daniel, then look at the card in my hands. On the front in a hand-decorated script are the words, 'We remember when …'. I pull each end, and in between are four pages with words all over them, written on both sides in all different styles of handwriting.

I remember when we went ice skating and you fell and bruised your arse.

I remember when you told me Bradley James kissed you in year six.

I remember when we went on the Zipper at the Easter

Show because you said you needed a reason to scream.

I remember when I fell in love with you.

There are so many more memories from so many people, all written out in front of me. Some of them I don't know about, but a lot of them I do, and as I twist and turn the card in my hands, reading the words, I remember when a lot of these things happened.

I close the card, smiling, and hand it to Daniel. Then I reach into the second sleeve and take out the contents. More notes, and amongst them, a photograph. The picture is of Josephine, Veronica, and Rachel. On the back is written, 'Bitches forever', and it makes me smile, because they all look so happy. It's one of the rare occasions I've seen Rachel smile. She should do it more often. She's beautiful. They all are, and I should tell them that.

I should tell all my friends things like that, because I never know when someone will be taken away from me again. I might not get the chance to tell the people I love that I love them.

"That's a nice photo," Daniel says.

"Yeah, it is."

I turn to him and hug him fiercely. Then I pull back and look up into his eyes. His lips are curled into a smile, and I feel my face mimicking his expression. He leans down and rubs my nose with the tip of his.

"You okay, Jess?" he asks.

"I think I am."

I stand on my toes and move my arms so they are wrapped around his neck, and I kiss him, not caring that we're standing on a public street for anyone to see. Daniel parts my lips with his tongue, and I fall into him,

our hearts racing between us.

He breaks our kiss and searches my face. "What was that for? Not that I mind."

"I love you, Daniel Sullivan," I say, before I can chicken out.

His smile widens, and he rubs my nose again with his. "I love you, too."

"Thank you."

He chuckles. "You don't need to thank me."

"Actually, I do." I say. "Because without you, I wouldn't be able to stand here where my sister died, and smile."

Dear Josie

Today I did two things. I talked to Jarred about everything, and I finally went to visit the site of your accident.

I'm going to tell you about the accident site first, even though it happened after I saw Jarred, because it has to do with Jarred in a way I'll also explain.

I never thought I would ever be able to go back to the place you died and be okay. But I was okay, and it was amazing. Yes, I cried, but Daniel helped me replace that awful memory I had of you trapped in your car with the beautiful memory of what you meant to so many people.

Mum and Dad had a cross erected, and every day since your death, people have been visiting that telegraph pole and leaving stuff for you. There are so many letters I still haven't read yet, but the ones I have I will keep forever.

So, I stood there with Daniel, and we read through a few of the tributes, and then we collected them, like Mum has been doing regularly, so I could take them home and put them with the others. I have two big shoeboxes full now, and I know that if I'm ever feeling down, or I'm missing you like crazy, all I have to do is search through that box

for a memory of you, and you'll be right here with me.

Now for Jarred. Daniel dropped me off at his place this morning because I needed to talk to him. Despite us not being nice to each other lately, it was really great. We cleared a lot of stuff up, and we cried together. I don't think I've ever seen Jarred, or any of the guys at school, cry. I mean, there's nothing wrong with a guy crying. Daniel cried the other day, too. I think it's awesome that Jarred felt comfortable enough with me to show how vulnerable he is. He's always been so broody and macho.

And it was nice to know there's someone else who has been suffering as much as I have, and I don't mean that in a bad way. I mean that it's nice to be able to share my grief with someone who understands what that grief is like.

We talked about you, and how he feels about everything that's happened. How I feel.

Now for the reason I told you about visiting the accident site first. I have to be honest with you and tell you about the envelope Jarred left for us. He said he dropped it off not long after you died, and he went back to get it the next day, but it was gone (courtesy of Mum). He thought I must have read it, but I didn't until yesterday. I didn't read anything anyone had left until a day ago. It stood out to me amongst all the others because it was the only envelope addressed to both of us. Everyone else has been leaving things only for you. But Jarred, he made a list, where he had written out all the things he hated about us.

Don't worry, it wasn't very long, but that list is what made me go and talk to him. It's what showed me how broken up about you dying he really is. We've agreed to be friends, because really, there is no other option. I could never be with him. It wouldn't work, because I can never fill your shoes. And he could never be with me, because I look like you.

It seems we had the same problem. Every time he saw me, he was reminded of you. And every time I looked in the mirror, I saw you. At first I struggled so much with that, because I felt such guilt over your death. But now, when I look in the mirror and see you in me, I feel like you've left me with the perfect memory.

You will always be the other side of me.

Your loving sister, Jess xxx

Acknowledgements

The Other Side of Me first came into the world way back in 2012. It has taken me six years to get Jessica's story completed, because Katie needed to tell her story first. She's selfish like that.

As always, there are people to thank ...

Katrina, you read the very first (incomplete) draft of *The Other Side of Me*, and I'm thankful for your input and suggestions. I hope you like how Jessica's story turned out.

Selina and Serene, your names are always going to be in the acknowledgements section of my books. Both of you are incredibly talented, amazing, and supportive women. I couldn't do this writing thing without you both by my side.

My husband, Brendon, thank you for your love and support, and helping me fix my writing desk. To my children, I love you, and I can't wait until you're old enough the read *All the Things*.

Finally, to my readers, thank you again for reading another one of my books. You are the reason I keep writing. I hope I'm the reason you keep reading.

About the author

K. A. Last was born in Subiaco, Western Australia, and moved to Sydney when she was eight. Artistic and creative by nature, she studied Graphic Design and graduated with an Advanced Diploma. After marrying her high school sweetheart, she concentrated on her career before settling into family life. Blessed with a vivid imagination, K. A. Last began writing to let off creative steam, and fell in love with it. She is currently studying her Bachelor of Arts at Charles Sturt University, with a major in English, and minors in Children's Literature, Art History, and Visual Culture. She now resides in the countryside on the mid-north coast of NSW with her family and a menagerie of animals.

Connect with K. A. Last

Website www.kalastbooks.com.au
Facebook www.facebook.com/KALastBooks
Instagram www.instagram.com/kalastbooks
Pinterest www.pinterest.com/kalast
Goodreads www.goodreads.com/KALast
Twitter www.twitter.com/KALastBooks

**Scan the code to subscribe to
K. A. Last's newsletter.**

Available Now

Is love really worth the fall?

THE TATE CHRONICLES

Scan for more information